A PRISON CH
DARTMOOR

Rickards, Clifford

General Books

www.GeneralBooksClub.com

Publication Data:

Title: A Prison Chaplain on Dartmoor;
Author: Rickards, Clifford
Reprinted: 2010, General Books, Memphis, Tennessee, USA
Original Publisher: London, E. Arnold;
Publication date: 1920;
Subjects: Crime and criminals; Crime; Criminals; History / General; Social Science / Criminology;
BISAC subject codes: HIS000000, SOC004000,

1

A PRISON CHAPLAIN ON DARTMOOR

PREFACE.

IN writing the following reminiscences of my twenty-five years' experiences in the Prison on Dartmoor I have had two objects in view: first, to interest my readers and excite their sympathy for a class of men who, although they are criminals, are not without their good points, as some of them have recently shown by their conduct in the late war. I was talking lately to an officer who was engaged in much of the heaviest fighting, and he told me that he had two ex-convicts in his company who were conspicuous by their bravery and readiness to volunteer for any dangerous duty. My second object is my own pleasure in recalling and transcribing the various incidents which, although now ancient history, are still vivid and interesting to me, as I hope the reading of them may be to others. They are all at least true, and if there are no revelations of secrets hidden behind prison walls it is simply because no such secrets exist, or if they do they are unknown to me.

For twenty-five years, day by day, and often all day long, I was in and out of the prison, in closest contact with warders and prisoners, and only on two or three occasions did I witness anything that called for interference. Sometimes the tact and good temper of the warders under most trying and provocative circumstances was surprising; but let the men speak for themselves in the following pages.

A very learned lawyer, on leaving the Law Courts, used to say, "That poor wretch who has just been sentenced might have been a better man than I if he had had my opportunities; " or, as our great poet writes, "If we all had our deserts, who would escape the whipping?:

CHAPTER I

FIEST IMPRESSIONS IT is a damp, depressing, muggy November afternoon, and I find myself and my wife in a wagonette toiling up the steep hill which leads from Tavistock to Princetown. What my wife's thoughts were, as she viewed the desolate moorland on either side, I do not know, but mine were anything but what you might suppose. I was going to real work, in which I had become greatly interested, and I was going to a little world, isolated, away from the madding crowd, and with miles of wild moorland, and rushing streams, which whispered, the former of snipe, plover and woodcock, the latter of salmon and trout. Arrived at our destination we are heartily welcomed by the host and hostess of the weather-beaten, gaunt-looking Duchy Hotel; my first glance as I enter the hall revealing various bunches of black game, and snipe, hanging from the ceiling of the hall.

After a very abundant dinner, and a pipe, I furrage out the bar parlour for a chat with my very genial landlord, who enlightens me upon local affairs and expresses the hope that I shall find my stay amongst them to my liking. Amongst other items of news he tells me that they are hoping to have the railway brought up to the town, which he thinks will vastly improve their supplies and bring them within an hour's ride of Plymouth.

So here we are at the Prison door, and at 7 next morning I take my first chapel service, and introduce myself to my convicts. This service, lasting about 20 minutes, is held every morning throughout the year, and although in summer time it is most refreshing in the sunlight and buoyancy of the moor air, throughout the winter it is quite a different thing; in the darkness, fog, and often snow, there is not much to admire in the files of spectral convicts marching across the yards into Chapel. But inside the seen changes, and all is bright, and as cheerful as brilliant gas (home made) can make it.

On this my first appearance, I endeavour to speak a few words suitable to the occasion, and remind them that I have come with good intentions: but that a good deal depends upon them and their intentions, whether I shall turn out of much service to them. Of course at first they will regard me with suspicion, as a paid Government official, but in time they will find that although I must be paid or I could not live, my time and service are to be spent, if possible, for their good.

I hoped by their indifference they would not drive me to do what I had just read of a prison chaplain having done in Russia. He found that he could not get on as a paid official, so he went out, and got himself convicted and sent back as a prisoner, and then living with the men and working with them, and sleeping amongst them, he found his influence amongst them was far greater. Well, this wasn't Russia, and as one could not follow his example without committing some serious crime in this country, they must take me as I was, or not at all.

Then after a concluding hymn, we all march out, they to parade and go off to their different works, and the Chaplain to take a short service in each ward (three) of the hospital and so home with a good appetite to breakfast.

Here then am I, instituted to the responsible 12 A CHAPLAIN ON DARTMOOR post of Chaplain to about a thousand criminals, to be their friend, adviser and spiritual teacher. Why of all things in the world, however did I get here? Just let me think. Sure I am of this, that when I was ordained some few years ago, if I had been shown into the future, and had seen what was to be my fate, I should have turned back and refused to take Holy Orders. If there was one appointment that I least desired it was that of a Chaplaincy in a Prison.

My first curacy was in a charming Midland parish where everything was done to make one's duties pleasant, and the people so kind and sociable that they did their best to spoil their curate by overmuch kindness. In such pleasant surroundings I was one day invited to a day's shooting at a well-to-do farmer's, close by my quarters, there to meet the Chaplain of one of our largest prisons, who was spending his holiday with my friend the farmer. I saw a good deal of him during his visit, and found him so agreeable and well informed that from my heart I pitied him, as I thought of his work and surroundings, and compared them with my own. How anyone could undertake such a duty passed my imagination. When some year or so later I met my friend the farmer driving over to see me, and learned from him that his friend the Chaplain had written to ask him to see me and persuade me to take a prison chaplaincy, and join him in the work, I had no hesitation in refusing, and at the same time telling him how much I pitied him who had such work to do.

In course of time, however, I was led by my Vicar and friends to reconsider the matter, and my Vicar very kindly promised not to fill up my place, if I liked to go as chaplain on trial, and if I found it so distasteful as I imagined, I could give it up and return to my curacy. " At least," he said, " give it a trial, it looks like a call."

I went, and never regretted the step, and was only sorry that when I had reached the appointed age for retirement, and felt no longer equal to the duties, it was necessary for me to retire, and it is worth recording that so far from any dislike to the work on the part of those who undertake it, the men who have taken my place when I have been absent on leave have almost without exception expressed a wish to be permanently appointed.

My first day on duty I can recall. After the 14 A CHAPLAIN ON DARTMOOR early service in Prison and Hospital, and breakfast at home, I return to the Prison, and first visit the Penal Cells, where there are perhaps 20 or 25 men under punishment for various breaches of rules, the same consisting of low diet and solitary confinement. Here also a short service used to be held every day, but this I took upon myself to abolish, as under the circumstances I thought it would do more harm than good. Each man is in a cell by himself, and to this cell there are two doors, an inner one of solid wood, and an outer one of iron bars, through which, when the inner one is thrown back, the prisoner can be seen and conversed with through the iron bars.

I found at first there was great reluctance on the part of the warders to open both doors, as the temper of the men under punishment is not always smooth, and is sometimes quite otherwise. An appeal to the Governor soon put this all right, and I was admitted within the cell unaccompanied by a warder, and although for 20 years I visited the men every day, only once did I have any cause to regret it, and that was in the case of a man who had worked himself into such a temper that he was not really responsible for his actions. He had been confined in a cell perfectly dark, and when I entered to get a better look at him I found him between myself and the door. He shouted and bellowed at me, and when I told him I wasn't deaf and he needn't shout, he said, "Look here, Chaplain, will you get me out of this? " I replied, "Don't be silly, you know I can't get you out of this, any more than I can get you out of prison."

Well then," he said, " take that," and gave me a smart blow full on the nose, which began to bleed rather badly. I had my hands in my top coat pocket, and did not return his blow, when after hitting me he turned away like a petulant child almost inviting a return. When I took out my handkerchief to staunch the blood, I said, "Whatever did you do that for, D.?"

Well," he replied, " why don't you get me out of this?"

When the warder, seeing my nose bleeding, came in, he unfortunately attempted the same with him, but came off a little the worse for the scrimmage. Before leaving, the prison orderly, who got me a bowl of water, said, "You ought not to have gone in to him. He has been carrying on like a madman all night. They ought to have told you."

16 A CHAPLAIN ON DARTMOOR

The next day I found my friend in a light cell, rather sorry for himself, and when I asked him how he was, without getting up from his seat he said, "How am I? Look at my head! " " No, no," I said, "Jemmie, look at my nose! 5! which was somewhat swollen. I tried to beg him off any punishment for his attack on me, but unfortunately for him he had struck two warders, and had to receive the due reward of his deeds. In many future interviews we became very good friends, and he often laughed when I told him not to do it again.

Usually the mornings are spent in one's office, looking over the letters and the petitions which the men have written the previous evening, and afterwards in visiting the men in their cells, where they have come for dinner and rest, from 11-30 to 1 p. m. We may, on the way, pause for a few minutes and watch them march past the Governor and Chief Warder, who check the numbers of each party, as the warder in charge of his party calls out the number, and announces " all correct." And what a sight is here, a thousand of England's criminals, and what a sadder sight does it tell of, the wives and children, left without father and husband!

Here we see passing the men whose names were in all the newspapers for murder, for forgery, for burglary and arson. There is hardly a crime unrepresented, nor a trade or profession without its follower.

And so we follow them within the portals of the various prisons, where each man makes for his own particular cell. We will give him time to eat his dinner before intruding. It is not required that you knock before entering, as he will hear your key in the lock, and know who is paying him a visit, and it is quite exceptional to meet with anything but a cordial welcome; usually he makes a pretence of dusting the only stool, and asks you to be seated. It is always a question that comes uppermost to one's mind when unlocking the door, What sort of a man shall I find within? One just glances at a small ticket over the door, on which is written the number and the name of its inmate, together with the number of capital or small letters, which mark the years of his various sentences. With this information we enter, and proceed to business. Naturally as a commencement, if one has not seen him before, one asks where he has come from, and what he has been doing to 18 A CHAPLAIN ON DARTMOOR get into trouble. Once I was rather taken aback by the man saying, "I wonder if you can guess, sir? " Well I did, and guessed right the very first time. When I describe the man perhaps you can do the same; if not I shall not tell you. To begin with he was the ugliest little man I think I have ever seen. Red hair, pock marked, one eye blind, the other with a slight squint, and a very ragged set of front teeth!

Here is another case of extreme dexterity in the art of pocket-picking. I had asked the man what he had got his three years for, and he had told me that it was for a great many cases of the above crime. Well," I said, "I never can understand how you manage to take things out of a person's pocket without being detected. I was wearing a buttoned-up pilot jacket at the time, and turning my face to the wall I said, "Now I am looking into a shop window. I don't believe you could get my watch without my knowing it." Almost before I had finished he said smiling, "But Ive got it "; displaying it on his open hand. " I haven't snapped it off the chain as I should have done in real business, as I thought you would not like it." I did not feel a touch. It was like magic.

On another occasion I got called to account by the Governor for encouraging an old prisoner to display his accomplishments. We had a man with many convictions who was returned to us again and again, but never for any very serious crime. One, I remember he told me, I think it was his first offence and was for " stealing a horse and cab." His explanation was that he picked up a living by minding the cabmen's horses whilst they went into the shelter for their dinner. Sometimes they paid him, at other times they ran into his debt. Once a cabman owed him 7s. 6d., which he would not pay, so my friend determined that he would pay himself, and when the owner went to his dinner he mounted the box, drove into the streets, and plied for hire until he had earned his 7s. 6d. Then he made his mistake, and instead of returning the cab to its original stand he deposited it on another rank, and took his departure! Well, he was an interesting old fellow, and when he was out of prison he tramped all over England, Scotland and Ireland, and informed me by letter where he was, and what he was doing. I always encouraged him in this, hoping my sympathy might help to keep him 20 A CHAPLAIN ON DARTMOOR straight. However, the last time he came back to us he was doing his first six months in solitary confinement, and worked all day at tailoring in his cell, with the door kept open, so that the warder walking round the gallery could see whatever took place in the cells. I was paying him a visit one morning, and amongst other things asked him how he managed to pick up a living when on tramp. Well," he said, "I go into a pub and ask the people there, Would they like a recitation? and then pitch them one of my staves. Then the hat goes round, and I get a trifle to carry on with." " What can you recite? " I asked him. " Well, I know some of the pieces from Shakespeare, or the scene from It's never too late to mend between the Governor, the Chaplain, and the Convict over the Pore Boy." " I should like to hear that," I said. " What, here? "-" Yes, if you don't make too much row! " He began, and did it all very well, but when he came to the altercation between the Governor and the Convict, the latter raises a knife and shouts, "Stand back, you villain." To emphasize this my friend picked up a large pair of tailor's scissors, and raising them over my head exclaimed, louder than was advisable, "Stand back, you villain! " The warder, passing the open door, naturally concluded that the Chaplain was being murderously assaulted, rushed in, collared my friend Tommy, and said he must report the matter to the Governor. My explanation was accepted, and no bad results followed, but the Governor said I must not bring about such scenes, or perhaps some day there might be a real assault, and the warder might think, it doesn't matter, it's only the Chaplain. Poor old Tommy is dead now, but for some years after we had both left prison, he to go into the Workhouse, and I to a Rectory in South Devon, once every year he walked from Sutton down to Devon to see me. He made a point of calling at the various vicarages on the way down and asking the vicars to write to me and announce his progress. This was, of course, a safe way of obtaining a trifle to help him on the way, and he was such an engaging old rascal that few could resist the appeal.

In addition to voluntary and unasked for visits, I had two large boxes placed in the chapel in which the men who wanted to see me could place a tin tally stamped with the number of the cell, which I collected after service and took back 22 A CHAPLAIN ON DARTMOOR to the owners. This would sometimes occupy the whole of the time for visiting, and leave none for unasked-for visits. Some men would ask again and again to see the Chaplain, on the most frivolous pretexts, and so waste all the time when other more important calls were waiting. There was one man at Portland, a pleasant plausible fellow of a companionable disposition, who neglected no opportunty to ask to see the Chaplain, until at last my colleague absolutely declined to be drawn. He warned me against the man, and told me the following.

He said, "I was passing his cell door only yesterday, and as he knows my footstep he called, Oh! Mr. H., I want to speak to you, do open the door! ' Too busy this morning, tell me under the door what you want. ' No, do open the door, I want to speak to you very particularly. Opening the door the next thing was, I must sit down as it was such a long time since I had called (only two days before). Well, now look here, my man, look at the number of names down in this book I have to see, and only about half an hour to do it in. Tell me at once what it is you want. ' Well first of all do you notice any difference in me? 'No. Not in my looks; don't you notice I have parted my hair the same as your reverence down the middle? No, don't go, Mr. H., I wanted to tell you many other things! " Exit Mr. H.

It is always with some misgivings that I say good-bye to my friends. When about to be released and sent out into the world, with a few pounds in their pockets, one feels that if as well as advice, as to their conduct, one could tell them where to go and get employment, there might be some prospect of their keeping out of prison, but when one knows how difficult it is for them to find work, and live honestly, and how easy it is to fall back into the old ways of crime, one cannot but feel sorry that the world is as it is, and the prison taint can never be quite obliterated.

I read one morning of the final scene at Newgate of three men who were well known to me, although two of them were Roman Catholics. " Within the sombre confines of Newgate prison the extreme sentence of the law was carried out yesterday morning on Alfred Milsom, aged thirty-three, and Henry Fowler, thirty-one, for the murder of Mr. Henry Smith at Muswell Hill, and upon William Seaman, forty-six, diver, for 24 A CHAPLAIN ON DARTMOOR the murder of John Levy and Sarah Gale, his housekeeper, in Turner Street, Whitechapel." The two former had been at Dartmoor some years, and were well behaved, and always cheerful and bright. The last was a very nice man to talk to, and the last piece of work he did before his release was to erect a swing in my garden for the use of our little girl. He had, I believe, made no secret of his intention to get even with this John Levy for having first instigated him to commit a robbery, and then betrayed him to the police so as to keep the whole of the plunder. Such men ought not to be let out of prison until there is some evidence of reformation. I knew a man who was under a heavy sentence for a murderous attack on the master of a workhouse, against whom he thought he had a grievance. Twice he assaulted this man, after completing each sentence of penal servitude, and on his release at the end of the second sentence he made no secret of his intention to attack him again. If I had been in that Master's place I should have thought it was hardly fair to loose a bloodthirsty rascal at me periodically, simply because he had completed five or seven years in captivity. It would be as reasonable to open the cage of a man-eating tiger because he had been in captivity a few years, or to turn a man out of hospital with an infectious disease before he was cured only because he had been in hospital for a few weeks. Here is another extract from a leading article in the Daily Telegraph on the report of the Directors of Convict Prisons on the effect of the treatment and behaviour of the men in prison. " But by far the most important testimony in (this respect comes from the Chaplain of Dart-" moor Prison, where perhaps the very worst of " our criminals are congregated, and where the " finest opportunity exists for studying their " manifold characteristics. The labour of whole " ministration has not fallen on his shoulders– " he has been assisted by various other clergy-" men, who have thus set an example which " might be imitated with advantage in other: penal establishments. The Dartmoor Chaplain " is convinced of the beneficial effect of prison " discipline, as long as the convicts remain under " its influence, but he does not consider that it "is of permanent benefit, either in deterring " them from fresh crime for fear of the punish-" ment, or by any reformation of character " which would lead them to like the habits of 26 A CHAPLAIN ON DARTMOOR

" industry, cleanliness, and order here enforced. " He looks to higher and holier influences for " the attainment of this desirable result. If f permanent good is to be accomplished, it can " only be by the power of Christ's gospel being: brought to bear upon their hearts at the same " time that the discipline of the prisoners is carried " out firmly, but with humanity and kindness. " It has been found possible to administer the: prison rules strictly yet kindly, and the " convicts show by their look and manner an " intense appreciation of their changed treat-" ment. Another good influence brought to bear " on them is the blessed influence of books. " The library comprises 4,000 volumes, and " repeated applications are made for encyclo-" psedias, popular educators, and histories, some-" times with such good results that a man will " have acquired the knowledge of French, "German, or Latin so well as to be able to read " with interest any author in those languages." There is always a great demand for the dictionaries, not only of foreign languages, but more so of English. Some will also turn their minds to the study of mathematics, and in one case I remember a man so far advanced that he almost outdistanced his instructors. He would be puzzled over some of the hard problems at the end of Colenso's Arithmetic, and when the schoolmasters failed to enlighten him he would try the assistant doctor, who was a mathematician, and the assistant doctor would appeal to me, and between us all we would arrive at the solution of the problem; but I have known the whole staff puzzled for days because a prisoner wanted to know the answer to the question regarding the intake and output of a certain cistern, or how many miles of wire could be drawn from a ball of such and such a size. To have pleaded ignorance would have been fatal to our reputation on other matters. If we did not know the answer, and how to solve it, what was our knowledge in other things worth?

There is no doubt that a good library is one of the greatest blessings to a prisoner. Most of the men can read, and those who cannot are taught. It is the greatest solace to a man in his cell to have the company of a good book.

Stone walls do not a prison make

Nor iron bars a cage, and, given a good book to feed the mind, half the torture of imprisonment is effaced for the time.

A liberal allowance is granted annually by the authorities for the supply of new books, and it is the Chaplain's responsibility to make the selection, both of educational and interesting volumes. To assist me in this, I always gave notice to the men in Chapel that I was about to do this, and if there were any books they wanted, they could write the names on their slates, and I would see what I could do to procure them. I also tried to improve their opportunities to obtain what they wanted. When first I went to Dartmoor I found the rule in force that only one book could be allowed at a time, and changed only once a fortnight. No distinction was made between educational books and others of a lighter kind, consequently there was little use made of any educational or religious books. This rule I enlarged by allowing two books at a time, one of an educational or religious character, and the other a novel or biography, and these might be changed twice a week. The effect of this was that all the books soon were in circulation, and the library was much appreciated. Of course some of the men were unreasonable, and if they could not at once obtain the book they wanted, were apt to complain, first to me, then to the

Governor, and finally by petition to the Home Secretary.

Great demand was made for the periodicals– Chambers 9 Journal, Sunday at Home, The Quiver, Popular Educator, and such like. Dictionaries, English and foreign, were in great request; likewise classical authors and practical teachers like the Tailor and Cutter. The distribution and checking of these gave my five schoolmasters something to do in the daytime, assisted as they were by a few prisoners as orderlies.

Some men were never satisfied. To oblige some of the better educated I often lent books from my own private library, and this did not always suffice. I remember one man–a great reader to whom I had lent several of my own books–wrote a petition complaining that he could not get the books he wanted, and when our Director came down he consulted me upon the matter; so I took him to the prisoner's cell and showed him the books the man had on his shelf; they were eleven in number, and he only ought to have had two according to the rules. " But, said the official, " this is more than the allowance, and some of them do not belong to the prison library; how is that? " " Well, sir," I said, 30 A CHAPLAIN ON DARTMOOR

" I have lent him more than I ought, and some from my own library, just to keep him quiet, as I didn't want him to trouble you gentlemen at the Home Office." I heard no more about it; and so we went on, doing all we could to encourage the men to improve their minds and relieve the monotony of their lives.

Curious requests were sometimes made by misreading or miswriting of titles. One that rather amused us was the demand for a book called " Less Miserable." We found on enquiry that it was Victor Hugo's " Les Miserables " that was meant. In English the title appeared to be just what a man in misery needed.

I have known men make considerable progress in learning a language with no other help than the book. Many studied French, with a view, I surmise, to transferring their activities to that country on regaining their liberty. Others learned to read a Latin author with wonderful skill. I remember" one man who asked me to change his Virgil for a Livy or some other author, but I said, "Can you translate the Virgil?: " Try me," he replied; " Ive read it through more than once." I opened the book haphazard, and put him on to the passage, and he translated it better than I could have done myself.

CHAPTER II.

THE PEISON OF LONG AGO

DAETMOOR–the moor on the river Dart–for many years was a terra incognita, a vraie Siberie, sparsely inhabited by a few squatters and peat diggers. It was little known, except to a few who traversed it on foot or horseback. There were no roads, as we understand them in these days, when motors cross the moor daily in ease and comfort. No railways nearer than Exeter; and everything was brought by water, but only to Plymouth, fifteen miles away. Little had been written about Dartmoor in those far-off days, and to the majority of Englishmen it was as little known as some of the countries in the heart of Africa at the present day.

And yet it had all the romance and attraction of a wonderful and little known region, close on the borders of civilisation. There were tales of pixies and mysterious lights seen by benighted pixie-led travellers; there were its stone huts 32 A CHAPLAIN ON DARTMOOK and tin streaming shafts and mines, its stone graves and other relics of far distant dwellers on the moor, who had lived their lives here, reared their families, and passed away, leaving signs of their skill and work in all quarters of the moor.

It was not till 1809 that the moor was awakened to life and activity, and its doors opened to scenes of tragedy and comedy. It was at that date that the Government, not knowing what to do with all their American and French prisoners of war, decided upon Dartmoor as the most suitable residence for the men from sunny France. The least consideration would have convinced anyone that a more unsuitable place, as regards their health, could not have been found in all England. The great prison, however, was built and 2,500 prisoners of war were marched up from Plymouth and established there, with a sufficient force of warders and soldiers to guard them, for whose accommodation a number of quaint barracks were erected just outside the prison walls.

Mr. Basil Thomson in his book, "The Story of Dartmoor Prison," gives a series of vivid pen pictures of this first Dartmoor Prison, and the life within its walls. " It was an overcrowded city, without women, with its own laws, its

THE PRISON OF LONG AGO 33 schools, manufactures, and arts; its workshops where coin could be counterfeited and Bank of England notes forged." It is sad to read of the sufferings and deaths of so many gallant men, whose only crime was that they did their duty fighting for their country. That many died and were buried outside the prison walls is evident from the bones and relics that are to-day constantly turned up in digging the gardens and fields adjacent to the prison wall. Buttons inscribed with the name and number of the regiment are frequently disinterred. An officer engaged some twenty years ago in charge of a party digging the foundations for the road leading down to the Black-a-Brook, told me that they dug through a mass of bones and relics yards deep. These were all reverently collected and deposited in a special cemetery, with a granite obelisk in the middle, inscribed " Dulce et decorum est pro patria mori." A curious incident occurred in my time in regard to this cemetery. It was carefully planted, and flowers were to be seen on all sides, and a party of gardeners constantly looked after it and the adjacent plot, which was the resting-place of the American prisoners of war who were also immured in the 34 A CHAPLAIN ON DARTMOOR prison. One day the garden party, when digging up one of the flower borders, struck the tops of some coffins, and the warder in charge came to the Governor for instructions. Nothing could be done for some time, as a heavy snow storm set in and put a stop to all gardening operations; but when, after some weeks, operations could be resumed, we went with the doctor and then found that the soil had been so washed away that the tops of the coffins were almost level with the surface. Six of them were raised, and opened, and nothing whatever was found in them, nor could the doctor detect any signs that there ever had been any dead body therein. Many conjectures were hazarded to account for this. It was agreed on all hands that empty coffins, where wood was so scarce, were not likely to be buried. Was it in connivance with the authorities that live men were carried out as dead, to enable them to effect their escape, or were the dead bodies disinterred by body snatchers and carried down to the hospitals at Plymouth? The latter seems the most probable. That the coffins were quite tenantless is the fact; the mystery is never likely to be solved.

THE PEISON OF LONG AGO 35 in the village, who remembered the time of the French prisoners, and told me of the market that was held weekly, just within the prison gate, when the small farmers and moormen brought their produce, consisting of chickens, butter, eggs and vegetables, to be purchased by the prisoners for cash or in exchange for articles made by them from bones or wood, or other materials. Some of them were exceedingly clever and artistic. The old man described to me the appearance of this market when the moor people and the prisoners mingled, and much buying and selling went on. There were other incidents that he remembered, when escapes were attempted, and when a serious mutiny occurred, which was not quelled without bloodshed, and additional soldiers were marched up from the Plymouth garrison. The wonder was that these mutinies were not more frequent considering that beyond a few duties within the prison there was no work to be done, and the prisoners had to fill up the day by gambling, quarrelling and fighting. It is said that some coining and printing of bank-notes were accomplished, but my friend said there was little of either done for want of materials, and that 36 A CHAPLAIN ON DARTMOOR for the most part the men loitered and loafed about the yards, until perhaps a fight or duel drew them to witness the combat.

The old man died before I left, after a short illness. I saw a good deal of him before his end came, and he was cheerful and happy to the last. It seemed curious to me to be brought into seeming contact with the scenes of those far-off days by converse with one who had seen and conversed with the French prisoners of war. The old man was over ninety years old.

There are inscriptions and letters and hieroglyphics on the outside walls which, if one could read their meanings, would no doubt reveal man a doleful and tragic tale. Some of them are almost illegible through the influence of time and weather, but others are still as fresh as when they were carved in the stone by some unfortunate exile. Other reminders of these captives are occasionally revealed. One day, as the men were engaged on some drainage repairs in the yard outside one of the oldest prisons, they all at once found the earth subsiding, and found themselves in a subterranean tunnel which led from about the middle of No. 4 Prison for many yards towards the outside prison wall.

THE PRISON OF LONG AGO 37 It was traced back to one of the cells in No. 4, and finished about half-way across the yard. It was evidently an unsuccessful attempt at escape, and must have taken many hours' hard work to accomplish. What brought it to an end before the boundary wall was reached? What was done with the earth that was excavated? It seems unlikely that it was stopped by any discovery, or the tunnel would have been filled in, and not left for the use of any future prisoners who might discover and complete the unfinished road to freedom.

By all accounts the Frenchmen were a rough and troublesome gang, and how they were stowed away and how they slept in prisons that now accommodate only a tenth of their number one can hardly imagine, and it is perhaps better left in mystery. That they should have quarrelled and fought and gambled is not surprising, and when peace was signed, and the gates were opened for their release, it must have been a happy day for those who had survived the hours of a long imprisonment, to depart from that which they described as a vraie Siberie to their own sunny France. It is said that the site on Dartmoor was selected for their internment 38 A CHAPLAIN ON DARTMOOR with a view to the impression it would make upon them of the climate and soil of the rest of England, so that on their return home, if the idea of a war with England was mooted, they would declare it was such a beastly land that it was not worth fighting for!

After their departure and the release of the American prisoners, the old prison was left empty and desolate; inhabited only by the bats and owls, until a company was formed to extract naphtha from the peat which was abundant in the adjacent bogs. This soon came to an end, and again the place was left untenanted. As an old inhabitant once told me, you could have a house or two if you liked, and no rent to pay.

The French officers were allowed to live in the neighbouring towns if they gave their parole, and mementoes of their sojourn and deaths may be seen in the churches at Moretonhampton and Ashburton and Totnes. In the centre aisle of the church at Moreton all the flagstones have inscriptions to the memory of Major or Colonel So-

and-so, of certain French regiments of the infantry and cavalry. I expect in life they made things lively in the towns, and they certainly left other reminders behind them, before their

THE PRISON OF LONG AGO 39 departure, in life or by death. I was once attending a warder seriously ill in the hospital, and before he died he asked me to make his will, leaving everything to his wife. Accordingly I made it in the name by which he was known to us, but when I took it to him for his signature, he said that the name I had written was not quite right, and by the addition of a letter or two it was turned from English into French. He told me that his father or grandfather, I forget which, was a French officer in captivity, and quartered at Ashburton, where he married an English wife. For reasons of his own he had changed his name into an English one.

CHAPTER III.

VISITORS–THE DAILY HOUND

THE Prison is like Bluebeard's chamber, in that it is closed, and not accessible to the public; so everyone wants to see the inside of it, and few there are who succeed, as without a permit from the Home Office admission is verboten. Until recent times almost anyone could obtain entrance, and a warder was detailed every afternoon to show visitors round, much as the beefeater at the Tower conveys the people round all the sights therein. As usual, it was chiefly by the abuse of this indulgence that the public themselves caused this privilege to be stopped, and all applications refused. It was generally rumoured that the last straw was a complaint from the Roman Catholic priest that he had found a large number of tracts scattered in his chapel, of a strong Protestant flavour, and decidedly anti-Roman Catholic. It was suspected, and enquiry confirmed the suspicion, that these tracts had been introduced by two well-meaning old ladies, who had been shown over the Prison the day before, and so, to stop such annoyances, it was thought best to stop all visiting for the future. Exceptions were made if good reason could be shown on the part of the applicant, and that he was prompted by something more than idle curiosity.

Still, in spite of this, we had usually in summer many visitors, and I have seen on various occasions, in that small and insignificant village, many whose names were well known in the world. The Duke of Edinburgh on one occasion paid us a visit, and seemed much interested in all he saw; he lunched at the Duchy, and after his departure there was a scramble for his oyster shells. Another well-known Captain of one of H. M. ships, on being shown round, was much interested in the kitchens, and after tasting a cup of cocoa such as was supplied daily to the prisoners, let out a little strong language, declaring it was superior to what was supplied to the men on his own ship. Then we had a visit from Lord Eosebery and our own member of Parliament, and in later days Mr. Lloyd George and Mr. Churchill, whose visit was chiefly 42 A CHAPLAIN ON DARTMOOR famous for the liberation by their influence of the man known on all the newspapers as the Dartmoor Shepherd, and who showed his gratitude by returning to the Prison shortly afterwards on a fresh conviction.

In fact, so frequently were we favoured by visits from the high and mighty, that at last we ceased to take much interest or put ourselves to any inconvenience to see them; but one day I found all the villagers on the alert, and evidently some very important arrival was expected. Upon enquiry, I was told that it was Fred Archer, the great jockey, who was expected; and when he drove through with his wife, whom he had just married, a more enthusiastic and noisy welcome was given him than had ever been vouchsafed to all the bigwigs who had preceded him. He looked so happy and jolly, as he drove through the crowd, that no one could have foreseen the sad end which was so near.

Amongst our most notable visitors was the late Sir Henry Acland, the great Oxford doctor, who came and spent several weeks in the village, and showed great interest in the prisoners and their welfare, both temporal and spiritual. He came to my office frequently, and chatted pleasantly over my work, and examined the large library of books provided for the men, enquiring as to their tastes and the kind of books most frequently in request. He cheered me much by his sympathy and advice, and I was very sorry when his visit came to an end.

The interest in our moorland establishment was evidently not confined tp present days, although when I first went to Princetown it was not much known to the outside public. Articles in the magazines, and books by well-known authors like Eden Phillpotts, have published to the world its charms, and many a man reading these over the fire in winter has said to his wife, "I think well go and have a look at Dartmoor next summer, my dear."

Still, even in the early days of Queen Victoria there were visitors. Palgrave writes: " Our " way lay right across Dartmoor, desolate and " eerie even under the brightest sun, to Prince-(t town, a village gloomy in itself from its high " and wind-exposed site, and more so from the " great convict prison, whose inhabitants we " saw working in sad files, and guarded by rifles " from escaping. The inn, rough and small but clean, was in accord with the surroundings.

44 A CHAPLAIN ON DAKTMOOR

" One bedroom, with two huge four-posters, was " allotted to us, and Tennyson lay in his with a " candle, reading hard the book which on his " trip he had taken for his novel companion, and " at every disengaged moment opened whilst " rambling over the moor. This chanced to be " one of Miss Yonge's deservedly popular tales,: wherein a leading element is the deferred " church confirmation of a grown-up person. " On Tennyson read, till I heard him cry with

" satisfaction, I see land! Mr.– is just

" going to be confirmed!– after which darkness " and slumber."

When I first arrived at Princetown the old inn was just as Palgrave describes it with its bedroom and four poster beds, and it is something to remember that one has slept in the same bed as Tennyson. Now that same small inn has become a fine hotel, with its electric light, baths and nice bedrooms. If you want good fare I advise you to go there.

A by no means infrequent request from friends was, "Could you get the bearer of this permission to see over the prison? He is much interested in the reformation of prisoners." This, of course, meant entertaining my friend's friend, and taking him round the place, which would entail the best part of an afternoon. Sometimes such a friend would be spending a few days on the Moor, and if he wore a white tie and could be inveigled into staying over a Sunday, his services might be utilised for the Chapel, and it was always my aim, as far as possible, to get a new man in the pulpit, if only that the men might hear a fresh voice and a better sermon.

In such a case, I might be asked if my friend might accompany me on the daily round and common task, and see all the details of a Chaplain's duties, perhaps with an idea that he might apply for such a post in the prison service. In answer to such a request I would consent, reminding him that early rising was the order of every day; the morning service being held at 7 o'clock, which meant turning out at 6 a. m. I got so accustomed to this early rising that I felt no trouble over it, but it was one of the greatest difficulties to one unaccustomed to it, and when I-went on leave, and a substitute was installed in my place, my last injunction always was, "Now don't be late or absent for morning prayers "; and on my return and enquiring how he had got on, the usual reply was, "Well, for the 46 A CHAPLAIN ON DAETMOOR first night or two I could not go to sleep for fear of not waking in time. I dozed off and woke up with a start, looked at my watch and found it 1 a. m., dozed off again, woke up, looked at watch, 2-30 a. m. Dozed again, woke at 4-30 a. m. Only one and a half hours more and then time to get up. Went sound asleep and when next I looked at the time found it 8 a. m."

One hour too late for chapel and only the Scripture Reader there to read the service. So at 6 a. m. I tumble out of bed and go and call my friend, telling him to hurry up, and if he likes, he can postpone his bath and shaving until we come back to breakfast. Lighting my Etna to warm up a cup of cocoa, while I shave and wash and dress, hurriedly swallowing the beverage and a roll, we sally forth into the fresh morning air, and make our way up to the prison gate, and demand admittance. The gatekeeper looks very breezy and wide awake, as he has only just relieved his duplicate, who has been on duty all night. He wishes me good-morning, as he hands me a bunch of keys, which are never allowed to be taken outside the prison gates, and if lost would entail the renewal of every lock in the prison. He opens the small gate leading into the yard, down which we proceed for some distance with flower beds on either hand, giving a cheerful look to the scene in the bright sunshine, which otherwise might be thought gloomy and depressing, with the large building and walls surrounding us. For here we are, inside the awful prison. How many sad feet have traversed this very path, coming in or going out of prison. If these walls could show us the photographs of all the notorious criminals who have paced up and down, what a picture gallery it would be, the Newgate Calendar enlarged, and very much enlarged! However, the bell is ringing out the last five minutes for service, and we overtake the men marching in single file from their various quarters into Chapel, as we proceed a little further through another iron gate to the Vestry, where we robe, and opening another door find ourselves face to face with eight hundred convicts seated on forms, with the harmonium and choir of thirty voices in the front, facing and close to the communion rails. The service opens with a hymn heartily sung by choir and congregation, followed by the lesson for the day and perhaps a few words in explanation, then prayers, another hymn and blessing, when all file out and proceed 48 A CHAPLAIN ON DARTMOOR to the adjacent yard to form into their different parties preparatory to marching off to their different places of work. " I notice," says my friend, " that you only used half the Litany this morning, and omitted several of the petitions."– " Yes," I said," the other half I shall say on Friday. We have not time for the whole, if we are to have the hymns and lesson; and I omit the petitions That it may please Thee to bless the magistrate, or that it may please Thee to bless the kindly fruits of the earth, and one or two other petitions which could hardly be expected would come from the hearts of men bleeding under the rigour of the punishment they were enduring for their past misdeeds." We watch the men as they march past the Governor and Chief Warder, who enters the number of each party as it passes and the warder in charge as he salutes calls out, "No. 2 Party twenty-two men, all correct," to be succeeded by party after party, until all have passed on or out to their respective work.

Then I and my friend go on through a big yard and a pleasant garden, all bright in the morning sun with an abundance of summer flowers, until we come to the iron gate which admits us to the hospital. Ascending the stone stairs we reach a landing, and on the right we enter an open door, at which stands the warder on duty. Entering, we find ourselves in a large, light ward, with a row of beds on either side occupied by patients. In the middle of the room there is a long table with two vases of flowers for ornament, and at this end of it a sort of lectern or prayer desk. Here, after wishing all good-morning, I take my place and conduct a short service, consisting of a short lesson from the Gospels, and a few appropriate words suitable to the occasion, followed by some prayers taken partly from the Visitation of the Sick, and collects and extempore prayers. A short visit, and a few enquiries at the bedside of each patient, and we pass out and enter a long ward with cells on each side, when a similar short service is held, and visits paid to each cell, all the doors being now open and the prisoners standing at each during the time of prayers. There is another ward downstairs, but the service here will have been taken by the Scripture Reader, so we may now take our departure to another part of the prison, and to the least pleasant duty of the day, viz., to the penal cells, where we shall visit each prisoner in his cell who is undergoing 50 A CHAPLAIN ON DARTMOOR punishment for some breach of discipline. Bread and water with solitary confinement do not improve a man's temper, but as they have no grievance against the Chaplain one enters each cell, and chats with the inmate. For the most part they are glad to see one, and are able to blow off a little steam, as regards their treatment by the warders for what they describe as a false report, and indignation because their word is not taken against that of their accuser. The men whom we find here are the same from time to time; the majority of the prisoners keeping clear of reports and punishment. In my diary I find an entry, "Said good-bye to G., who is to be discharged to-morrow. He has been twenty years in prison and has not had a single report for misbehaviour during all that time." It is here that the warders in charge have often a difficult task in dealing with the men, and they are picked officers, known for their tact and good temper.

Having finished here we will now go home to breakfast, which we feel. that we deserve after two hours on duty.

After breakfast my friend says he should like very much to see the workshops, so I conduct him first to the ground floor of a large building, which is one of the old prisons which were used long ago for the French prisoners, and bears the mark of age on its heavy walls. Inside it has been renovated, warmed and lighted by enlarged windows. Here seated at separate small desks are a large number of men, busy at shoemaking, or being taught by a warder how to sole and heel. This is a party much sought after, and prized; chiefly because it is an indoor job, and they are sheltered from the weather all the year round. We examine some of the work, and to our inexperienced eyes it seems very good, and equal to any first-class bootmaker's outside. Of course all the boots and shoes can only be for warders and convicts, or other of His Majesty's servants, as no work done by prisoners can be sold in competition with outside work, and this applies to all articles manufactured in our prisons.

We leave the bootmaking and ascend some wooden steps leading up to the tailor's shop. The first time I ascended here, at the very entrance, just inside, there was a large sewing machine, and working it a big man whom I at once recognised as the famous claimant whom I had last seen in Westminster Hall during the time of his famous trial. We look round, and 52 A CHAPLAIN ON DARTMOOR notice the men all diligently at work, sitting on the various tables tailor-wise, and all in silence, except for a word or two from the attendant warders. Before leaving we are shown by the master tailor some of the best garments, made entirely by the men around us. These are tunics and trousers beautifully sewn and splendid in their facings of gold lace, to be worn some day by chief warders or other big pots in our various prisons. Our next shop is the carpenter's, and here we notice that the majority at work are young men, some almost boys, whom we think ought never to have been sent to a convict prison, and who are now sent to the Borstal Institution and kept apart from the old and habitual criminals. However, on our visit they all appeared bright and cheerful, and except for their dress one would have thought we were in an ordinary busy workshop. Here was sawing and planing and hammering, while doors and windows were being turned out in large numbers to be used for the new warders' quarters which were being built in the village. After chatting to a few of the men and examining their work, we pass on, and just round the corner come upon the blacksmith's shop and a large number of smiths fashioning gates, posts, tyres for wheels, farm implements, and horse shoes.

And now the prison bell reminds us that it is time to clear off, and that all the men are about to march back to their cells for dinner, where they will be from 11-15 to 1 p. m., and where I, too, must be, as this is one of the few opportunities I have for visiting privately each man in his cell.

As we pass out of the main gate we meet party after party returning from their outside occupations, some from the bogs, some from the farm, some from the village, known as the cleaners, and some from the quarries; verily a mixed multitude, but all marked and plastered with the broad arrow as a sign that they have done things they ought not to have done, but at least this morning they have not been allowed to leave undone much that they ought to have done.

So home to lunch, and a pipe, and after an hour's rest we start afresh not into but outside the prison walls, where we shall see many parties at work reclaiming the moorland, and making it bring forth abundantly, in turnips, barley, and oats; others digging in the gardens to supply the prison with vegetables which, though a few weeks 54 A CHAPLAIN ON DAKTMOOR late, for the most part are abundant, especially celery, which the soil and climate appear to suit. We pass round the outside walls, and skirt the two cemeteries, one containing the bodies of the French, the other of the American prisoners of war, with an obelisk erected to the memory of the unfortunate men who died in captivity, an inscription on each with the Latin phrase, Dulce et decorum est pro patria mori. As we pass I point out to my friend the exact spot where the empty coffins were unearthed, as narrated in a previous chapter.

Passing on we lean over a wall and view the scene in the valley. The various parties are all at work, with the warders mixed up with them, both instructing and supervising them in their tasks. It seems a little risky to be cheek by jowl with a lot of men armed with pick and shovel, or other tools, a sudden blow from which would be fatal, but it is very seldom that anything of the kind happens. I once asked a warder if he did not feel nervous when passing close by a prisoner, who, perhaps, he had been obliged to report for some shortcomings in his work. He said they never thought about it, and if they did, and got nervous, it was time to give up the job and retire; but as a fact they were so used to the work, and knew the men so well, that they never thought of any danger, and so were quite unconcerned.

At some distance from the parties, but surrounding them, are seen the Civil Guards standing as sentries, some on the walls, some in the open fields, and others in the various lanes or roads. These guards are all armed with carbines, loaded and to be fired in case of a man trying to escape, but they are instructed to fire low and as far as possible avoid killing the man. My friend enquired of me if they were good shots. " Some are, I believe," I said, " but they get so little practice that I am not surprised if they miss."

I remember the case of a man who bolted in a fog from the gas works, and when he was captured and brought back I asked him if he was hurt by the shot which had been fired. He replied that he was nearly a mile away when he heard the rifle fired. This meant that the warder in charge did not miss him for a quarter of an hour after he had gone, but when he did miss him, he fired his rifle as if he had seen the escape.

But why not practise them at a target?

56 A CHAPLAIN ON DARTMOOR

Well, I only remember one occasion when that was done on the advice of a new military Deputy Governor, who had some wooden targets in the shape of convicts made and placed against the garden walls. He took some of the Civil Guards down and gave them a little target practice, when the parties were all about at their work. It was thought that this might have a deterrent effect on the mind of any man who thought of running away. They wasted a good deal of ammunition without much damage to the wooden convicts. It might not have been from what the real convicts saw and thought of the performance, but perhaps was only a coincidence, but it is a fact that next day five men made the attempt and were brought back uninjured! If there was any more practice with the rifle it was done less openly or when the convicts were not near.

Now as we lean over the wall I say to my friend: Look down there to where this road turns at right angles a quarter of a mile away; that is Park Corner, and is so labelled by a printed board. It is not much like the Park Corner we associate with all the traffic of London. There is no congestion here of tram cars and taxies, and pedestrians hurrying into the Park, but just the bare roads, with stone walls on each side, and a few sheep grazing in the fields, and rabbits feeding by the walls; and yet not long since it was the scene of a real tragedy. A party of convicts were being marched into the prison for dinner and a slight fog was flitting across, when all at once a half-dozen men broke from the ranks and leaping the walls made for the open moor. Some were captured by the attendant warders, but as they showed fight were rather unceremoniously dealt with, and one man was fatally shot. I met the bearers bringing him into the prison, and, removing the handkerchief from his face, I saw that he was dead. The others made good their escape for a time, but were soon caught and returned to the prison, except one man, whose adventures I have already narrated, who got as far as Devonport, where he was recognised, owing to the sagacity of a dog, who persisted in barking at him, and so called the attention of a policeman to the wandering minstrel, for a minstrel he was, as his poem describing his adventures proved. It was a difficult situation for the few attendant warders when this emeute took place. They were a quarter of a mile from 58 A CHAPLAIN ON DARTMOOR the prison, and if any of them went in pursuit of the runaways, the guard would be so weakened that the rest of the men might follow the example that had just been set them. They did the wisest thing, and marched the party straight to the prison, and then set off with others in pursuit, and soon brought in all but one of the six who had bolted.

When a death occurs in the prison from whatever cause, a Coroner's inquest is always held, and the cause of death enquired into. Naturally in a case like the above, the warders responsible for the shooting are a bit anxious as to what the verdict may be, and if any friends of the deceased make their appearance, they are curious to know in what light they will regard the shooting of their friend for running away. I remember such a case when a very desperate convict had been shot. He had been convicted and sentenced to a long term of imprisonment for breaking into a woman's house, and because she would not reveal to him where her money was, he deliberately forced her on to the fire. I forget how it was that he was killed, but I think he brutally attacked the warder and in trying to escape was shot. When his friends appeared on the scene, some of the warders got into converse with them, and amongst remarks of condolence for them in their sorrow at the loss of their brother or uncle, or whoever it was, explained how sorry they were that in the course of duty they had been obliged to fire and most sorry that the shot was fatal. Well, to their surprise the answer came, "If you are sorry we are not; in fact it was the best thing that could have happened, and we were very glad. Our only sorrow would have been if he had lived long enough to come back to us."

It is now late in the afternoon, and soon it will be time for the parties to return to the prison for their tea, so we will go up to the prison yard and see them march in past the Governor and the Chief Warder, when their numbers are again checked as we saw when they marched out. What a spectacle it is of humanity in its most pitiable form. For here pass before us over a thousand men convicted and sentenced to this life for every crime that men can and do commit. And this is the reward of their misguided inducement to break the law, thinking that it will be for their well-being. I once quoted from a newspaper the average gain in money on the part of a number of murderers, and I think it averaged 60 A CHAPLAIN ON DARTMOOK about 30s., and for this they had slain their fellow-man and forfeited their own lives. And in lesser crimes I pointed out, and, as I thought, proved, that crime does not pay, and honesty is the best policy, regarded only from a business point of view. Think of any gains you may have made by some successful robbery, I said. Put the amount on one side of the account, and on the other the value of your daily work as a prisoner. Say your sentence is only five years, and that your work, the labour of your own hands, is worth only 2s. per day, and on which side is the balance? You will see that it does not pay to be a thief.

I was somewhat taken aback when one of my hearers disputed this, in a talk I had with him in his cell, declaring that very often burglary paid better than any other profession, and that he knew a man who owned two sides of a street, which he had purchased with the proceeds of successful burglaries. I doubted this, but reminded him of the saying that exceptions prove the rule, and that sooner or later the criminal is bound to be caught. The first success will be only an encouragement to go on, and the more he succeeds the more careless he becomes, until at last he is sure to be caught, and the payment has to be made in the suffering of years of imprisonment. But here are the various parties marching past us in step, and looking cheerful now another day's work has been done, and they are one day nearer the end of their sentence. There is hardly a trade or profession that is not represented in this passing crowd, doctors and lawyers, clerks and schoolmasters, jewellers and watchmakers, carpenters and electricians. Whatever need may arise in our daily life, I think it could be remedied by the skill or knowledge of the men passing before us. One man told me that if he were allowed, he could instal the electric light throughout the prison and generate enough electricity from the water power close at hand.

They pass into the various prisons each to his own cell, where they will receive the cocoa and bread allotted for supper, and after giving them time to eat this, and tidy up their cells, I avail myself on most evenings of the opportunity to pay them a friendly visit, in the privacy of their little homes, and hear a good deal concerning the past and advise as to the future. On this evening I am unable to do this, as I am engaged just now in the quarterly examination of those 62 A CHAPLAIN ON DARTMOOR attending school, and it is my duty to examine separately each scholar, and see what progress, if any, has been made since my last examination. Here on the ground floor of the big prison, seated at forms and desks, are about fifty men of various ages and capabilities. Some are so young that one wonders how they have escaped the attendance officer outside and have come to us unable to read or write. This we soon remedy, except in the case of three or four who appear quite hopeless, and after perhaps a year or two have to be given up, and dismissed as unable to learn when four or five schoolmasters have done their best to make them.

I take first the top class, who have the benefit of perhaps a year's teaching, and examine each by hearing him read from the sixth standard, and marking him accordingly, in the hopes of being able to excuse him from further attendance at school, a hope which he reciprocates and will therefore do his best to accomplish. With the next lot it is different, and a little tact and persuasion are necessary to get a response. I am standing by the table at which the men are seated, and as I call out each man's name he stands up, and reads, where the last man left ofi.

All has gone smoothly so far, and each man has read and sat down. Now it is Smith's turn, but when I call his name there is no response, and when I find him nothing will induce him to stand up and read. Perhaps he is in a bad temper, and thinks he has some grievance, or perhaps he wants to show off before the others, so we must be careful and if possible avoid ructions. " Come now, Smith 5 I say, " don't be foolish. It isn't often you know that you read to me. Do it now just to let me see what a good fellow you have been, and what progress you have made since I last heard you, when you read so nicely."

But no, he still remains obstinate, and I pass on to the next man, who promptly jumps to his feet, proud to show what he can do. Well, Smith, Ive got another class to examine, and then Ill come back to you, and hope to find you ready to oblige." After about a quarter of an hour I return, and repeat the order, "Smith, stand up and read." Still no response, and now one of the warders has drawn near to see what is the matter. Instead of repeating the order aloud, I pass round the end of the desk to where Smith is sitting, and with my hands on his shoulders, I say in his ear, "Now Smith, don't be a fool, and 64 A CHAPLAIN ON DAETMOOR compel me to report you, a thing I have never had to do before. Perhaps you are tired, so Ill excuse you from standing, but read you must, or take the consequences; so now just go on here "; and I put my ringer on the place, still leaning over him. Generally this succeeds, and he makes the attempt, reading out just a line or two. This is sufficient for me, as I feel we are on ticklish ground, and I am glad to end the business without giving the warder the necessity of reporting the scholar. I do not remember any case in all my examinations where I have failed in the end to get the reading done, and all part friends.

And now school is over, the desks and forms are carried away, and the men return to their cells and get ready for bed, as all lights are out at 8 p. m., and the prisons closed for the night. The hard work and the early rising have made all ready to turn in, and I don't think we have many cases of insomnia, but all these criminals sleep the sleep of the innocent, and there is neither nightmare nor groans nor snores to be heard through the long hours of the night. All are sleeping the sleep of a little child and no ill dreams appear to disturb their rest.

CHAPTER IV.

NOTABLE PRISONERS

BEFORE leaving the prison there is just time before it closes to pay a visit to the Infirmary, and minister to any serious cases, and so possibly avoid a call later in the night, if any are taken worse. I go into the open ward, where there is a case of a young man seriously ill, and seating myself by his bedside I ask how he is feeling, and express a hope that he is better than when I saw him in the morning. Would he like me to read to him? Yes, please, is the answer in a most ingratiating tone, and so the reading and a few prayers finished, I sit by his bed and enter into a quiet chat with him. Amongst other topics we naturally drift to his past life, and what brought him to Dartmoor. He is a pleasant looking young fellow, with no sign of a criminal about his face, and you would, from his rosy cheek and smiling eyes, take him for a well-nurtured youth who had lived all his life in the country 66 A CHAPLAIN ON DARTMOOR in healthy surroundings. " Tell me," I ask, " what have you done to get here? " I committed burglary," he replied, " not once, but a good many times, and got caught at last." " You don't look like a burglar, nor like one of the criminal class," I said. " No, perhaps not, but if you look at my record youll see I am one of the best, or I ought to say the worst, burglars in London."

Here is no Bill Sikes, with the bullet head and cruel beast-like features, such as we meet with in pictures and detective stories, but a quiet, placid, and pleasant-featured youth, such that if you found him in your house at midnight, you would be disposed to think he was the gentleman from next door who had come in by mistake, rather than a burglar intent on robbery. Appearances are deceptive, and I must dispute the conclusions of Lombroso, who declared, after long study of prisoners and prisons, that all criminals could be identified and classified by their abnormal appearance. Thick woolly hair, shifty eyes, bushy eyebrows, a nose defective in shape, ears outstanding and prehensile, skin pale and wrinkled, a receding chin, and a protruding upper jaw. He went further than this, and pretended that lie could tell at a glance what crime the man had committed. Murderers can be known by a deficiency in their frontal curve, combined with a receding forehead; thieves by their enlarged orbital capacity and bulging forehead; sexual offenders by their bright eyes, rough voices, swollen eyelids and lips, and occasionally by the fact that they are humpbacked. The eye of the homicide is glassy, cold and fixed, while the forger has generally a clerical appearance and singular air of bonhomie. Such is the argument which Lombroso called criminology, and which he got many people to believe, until his whole science (so-called) had the bottom knocked out of it by Dr. Goring's research and his work called " The English Convict," which, for my part, after twenty-five years of intimate association with criminals, I unhesitatingly confirm. The result of Dr. Goring's inquiry establishes the fact that there is no such thing as a criminal type at all. He says truly that the criminal is differentiated by inferior stature, by defective intelligence, and to some extent by his anti-social proclivities, but that, apart from these broad differences, there are no physical, mental, or moral characteristics peculiar to the inmates of 68 A CHAPLAIN ON DARTMOOR

English prisons. I think Dr. Goring's conclusions are true and that Lombroso's, in schoolboy phrase, are tommy rot.

St. Matt, xxvii, 16: " They had then a notable prisoner."

One was always interested and a little curious to see what manner of man he would be whose trial and conviction had filled columns of the daily papers. And in an interview after his arrival at the prison, the first impression was one of surprise to find that he was very much like other people, both in appearance and conversation, so that it was hard to realise that this was the individual guilty of such a crime, and I have no doubt it was the same with Barabbas, alluded to in the text by St. Matthew. A notable prisoner guilty of insurrection and murder, and pardoned instead of the innocent Saviour. I wonder what he was like and what was his appearance. For we have some notable prisoners here (at Portland). Here is an extract from my private diary:

" March, 1877.–Off Chapel duty this morning, as my colleague takes the duty alternate weeks with me. I accordingly enter the prison a little earlier to take the service in the penal class prison, meeting the men starting for Chapel as I cross the yard. First comes H., the American imprisoned for life, with the other American forgers, M. and B., who (as I shall tell later) succeeded in drawing 70,000 from the Bank of England by forged bills of exchange and cheques. This man is specially guarded, as large sums have been offered as bribes to get him out of prison. Next come two or three cripples, men with wooden legs. Then a succession of men in close order, two and two abreast, with a warder at intervals. Then I meet two notable prisoners, Melody and Shaw, the Fenians, under sentence for life. Last of all comes a batch of black dressed men, some with leg irons, showing that they are violent and have been guilty of assaults upon the warders. These are closely guarded by warders with fixed bayonets, and are being taken to the oakum shed, where they will spend the day, much to their disgust. As they pass me I receive a smile of recognition from several special friends.

" As I want to see the Governor, I step into his office in passing, and find him at this early hour busy amongst his papers. The office is a nice large room, carpeted and well furnished.

70 A CHAPLAIN ON DARTMOOR

Maps on the walls, a large writing table with many drawers. The windows overlook the yard I have just crossed, and a good view is obtained of the quarries where most of the prisoners work. On the left hand, where the Governor usually sits, I notice the telegraph disc with wire leading to the Verne Fort, with the varying signals for calling for the soldiers stationed there in case of fire, mutiny, or escapes. On the right hangs a revolver ready to hand in case of an unexpected assault by some frenzied prisoner. Over the mantel shelf hang a few photographs of notable prisoners; also one of a man strapped to a chair and making hideous faces, because he objects to having his photograph taken. There is also another good likeness of S., the Fenian Head Centre, once a guest here. There is also on a sideboard a wonderful collection of things not usually seen on such a beautiful piece of furniture. I ask the Governor what they are? Oh, those, he said, are the various weapons that have been used by convicts in committing various assaults. Stones tied up in handkerchiefs, hammers stained with blood, large pieces of granite, spades, pickaxes, etc."

most notable prisoners. First of all we had Michael Davitt, whose likeness in his convict dress I still have in my album. He was rather morose and sullen, but on the whole gave little trouble and seemed as though he had made up his mind to make the best of a bad business until he got released. I saw little of him, as he was a Roman Catholic, and soon after my arrival at Dartmoor he was removed to Portland. The Chaplain there called on him soon after his arrival, and asked him if there was anything he could do for him? Any particular books he could send him? Would he like, for instance, a good History of Ireland? " No, thank you," he said, with a smile, "I think I know enough on that subject." He was released shortly afterwards, and wrote a book on his prison experiences. Then we had the great Sir Roger T., great in two senses, as a notability and as the heaviest and biggest man we had ever had in our care. He and the doctor were always at loggerheads, chiefly, I think, owing to the fact that our kindly doctor did not supply stimulants to the extent he could, and therefore ought, to men who had been accustomed to their bottle a day under happier circumstances. For some reason or 72 A CHAPLAIN ON DARTMOOR other, he was removed shortly after my arrival to Portsmouth, and was delighted at the prospect of being under another doctor, more amenable to his wiles, but his satisfaction was shortlived, as our doctor soon afterwards followed him to Portsmouth. Of course, amongst some of the prisoners he was held up as a martyr, and an example of the injustice of our criminal laws, but the majority took a different view, and regarded him as an impudent imposter, and he did not improve matters by his stand-off manner and contempt for his fellow prisoners.

I once was visiting a very intelligent man in his cell, and somehow the conversation turned on Sir Roger. This man told me he went to school with him at Wapping, and knew him afterwards as Orton the butcher. I asked him if he had any doubts about him. " Not the least doubt in the world; he is Arthur Orton I am certain." " Did you ever get a word with him? " I asked. " Yes, soon after he came here, I addressed him as an old acquaintance and reminded him of our school days, but he wouldn't own to it, and shut me up."

I also came across another man connected with the imposter, Jean Luis, the mate of the steamer which was supposed to have taken Sir Roger to Australia. He also told me that the whole thing was a fraud, and they only got what they deserved. Sir Roger's confession in later days confirmed the veracity of these two men.

Then we had at Dartmoor for many years Mcdonnell and Bidwell, the great bank swindlers, who managed to draw 70,000 from the Bank of England by what seemed the most simple and easy artifice. They were men of very different character. Mcdonnell was an intelligent and gentlemanly prisoner, who gave no trouble, and worked steadily at his task. Bidwell, on the other hand, could ill brook the irksomeness of prison life, and was constantly in trouble for some minor infringements of the rules. As he was often under treatment in the Infirmary, I saw a good deal of him. He often asked my opinion about his chance of getting a mitigation of his long sentence (life) and I always told him there was no chance so long as the greater part of the plunder was unaccounted for. He was released after many years and returned to the bosom of his family, and there wrote a book, "Forging his Chains," describing the conception and execution of their successful swindle. His 74 A CHAPLAIN ON DARTMOOR chief excuse was the great temptation to dishonesty afforded by the facility with which they discovered it could be accomplished. It was very simple. They managed by some means to get possession of one or two genuine bills of exchange on some well-known city firms. These they paid in to a branch bank of the Bank of England to the account of B."s younger brother, which he had opened under a fictitious name, and it was the discovery of this man's pass book with a small balance which first put the idea of the swindle into their heads. The first genuine bills being accepted and a credit given for the amounts to this account, they then forged the names of other prominent firms for still larger sums, and paid them into the credit of the same account. Whether the bank officials made any enquiry of the firms whose signatures were on these bills is doubtful, but if they did so in regard to the first two or three bills they would learn that they were genuine, and would be met by payment at the end of the three months when they fell due. This no doubt lulled all suspicion, and led to their neglect to make any enquiry in regard to the others sent in later, and which were clever forgeries of the names they bore.

At the same time they proceeded to send in cheques for various sums in cash, by the hands of a man named N., who was the only man to appear on the scene, the two principal forgers never being seen, except by people at the Langham Hotel, where they took up their residence and fared sumptuously every day. The cheques presented were always honoured, as of course by the bills constantly paid in, and credited to the account, there always appeared to be a substantial balance to draw upon. N. told me himself that no matter whether the cheque he presented were for a large or small amount, and sometimes it was for thousands, the only question he was ever asked by the cashier was, "How will you have it? " It seemed to the conspirators that the Bank of England was at their disposal, and they had only to dip their hands into its coffers and they could take what they liked.

Of course they knew their time was limited to three months, when the bills, both genuine and forged, would fall due, and the whole thing would be exposed, but a good deal can be done in three months, and long before that they had drawn from the bank over 70,000. B. told me they intended to clear out when they obtained 76 A CHAPLAIN ON DARTMOOR.

another 20,000, which appeared so easy and so modest. But as in the case of most crimes, there is always that one little mistake which leads to the undoing of the scheme. The clerk as usual appeared one day with another bill drawn, I think, on Baring's, and it was taken over by the cashier as usual, without any scrutiny, but when the Chief Cashier saw it, he noticed a slight omission in the date; the month and year were all right, but the day of the month was absent. He pointed this out to the cashier, who said he would give it to the clerk when he came again, which in all probability would be in the afternoon. "No, no," said the Chief, "send it down to Baring's by messenger, and ask them to fill in the date properly." Accordingly it was dispatched by the hand of a confidential clerk, and as soon as it reached the officials at Baring's, they at once saw that it was a forgery. They pointed this out to the clerk, and asked if they had any more of the same kind? ' Heaps," said the clerk. So the fat was in the fire, and N., the supposed clerk of the forgers, was arrested when he appeared at the bank, but he refused to give any information about his employers. All the authorities knew was that the man himself, being an American, in all probability his employers were of the same nationality. It was not much of a clue for the detectives to start on, but the culprits themselves admired their ingenuity. They began by making enquiries in the Haymarket, Richmond, and other pleasure resorts, if any Americans had been spending lavishly over wine and women, rightly surmising that money in such abundance being so easily obtained would be as easily spent. This had been the case, for as one of them told me, they had lived like the rich, and spent like princes; so that very soon the detectives got a description of the two men they wanted. In the meantime one of them got away and boarded a ship sailing for America, but was arrested, and the other told me he got over to Ireland, and thought he was perfectly safe, as they had never been seen at the bank. He was at a hotel in Kilkenny, smoking his after-dinner cigar in the smoking room, when two gentlemen came in who were talking about the great bank forgery. They asked him if he had seen the evening papers, and tossed one over to him. There he read of the arrest of his confederate, and a full description of himself as a man very much wanted by the police. He told me that he didn't waste 78 A CHAPLAIN ON DARTMOOR much time in Kilkenny, but got away to the north and crossed over to Scotland, where he got a lodging in Edinburgh. Here he lay low for some weeks, only venturing out after dark, but as the hue and cry began to die down, he thought he might safely go to the end of the street where he could obtain the morning papers. This he did regularly for some days, and of all foolish subjects, as he acknowledged, he got discussing the matter with the proprietor of the shop. One morning the man's wife was present, and as soon as he had left the shop she said to her husband, "Do you know (or ken) I believe that's the other man the police are seeking."–" Nonsense," said the husband. They looked up the photograph and description, and came to the conclusion that it would be as well to inform the police, which they did; so that on his next appearance he was arrested, and in due time arrived at Dartmoor, where he spent a good many unhappy years. After his release he wrote me several letters from America, with an urgent appeal for my photograph and also one of the Governor of the prison, if I could obtain it. He afterwards sent me a copy of " Forging His Chains," but neither picture found a place therein, for the best of reasons. It is some years since I heard from him, and so conclude that he is not alive to-day. If he is, I wish that his latter days are happier than those in which I knew him.

Another notable prisoner was B., the great Turf Fraud manager, with his two confederates, the brothers K., all three very nice men to talk to, and not at all like the usual convict class. They all behaved remarkably well as prisoners, worked well, and gave no trouble.

B., the chief culprit, was a well-educated man, and could speak several languages. He took up his abode in the Isle of Wight, under the title of Prince W., and was soon on visiting terms with some of the 61ite in the island; he was entertained and f ted to his heart's content as a distinguished and attractive personality, to which his ingratiating manner contributed.

He and his confederates devised a scheme called the " Insurance Turf Betting," which held out to the public the almost certain results of their betting. It was a clever device, and on the face of it very attractive, and the success was marvellous. B. told me that every post brought hundreds of letters, with cheques for large sums of money, and from people one would never have 80 A CHAPLAIN ON DARTMOOR believed capable of taking a hand in what they must have known to be a shady transaction. Sufficient explanation had to be given to the investors to assure them of the certainty of winning, and if this were the truth, then it was little short of robbery to make a bet which must take money out of the other's pocket without any chance of his winning. A certain Countess De Goncourt sent them very large sums of money, and still wanted to send more, but in order to do so she was compelled to raise more capital on a mortgage of her property, and to this end was obliged to consult her legal adviser for the first time. The lawyer on learning the large amount she had already invested became suspicious, and strongly advised her to have nothing more to do with the Turf Insurance. She became indignant and pointed out to him the certainty of doubling her fortune by these investments. Becoming somewhat mollified by his arguments, she promised to wait the result of his enquiries before making any further investments. The result of his enquiries was that the chief agents thought it advisable to disappear with the large booty they had in hand. The two K. s found a safe harbour in New York, where they resided for some months, until they thought they might safely venture back to England. New York was becoming too hot to be comfortable for the following reason, told me by one of the K. s himself. With the proceeds of the turf fraud they had plenty of money in hand, and had no need to invent further schemes to plunder the unwary, but after some time, and a good time too, the pleasures of idleness and luxury began to pall on their active minds, and they wanted something to do to fill up the time of their exile in a foreign land. Accordingly they looked about them and concocted the following scheme pour passer le temps.

K. explained to me the fact that if you want to impose upon A., you must first get A. to believe that he is imposing upon you. When this is done the rest is easy. This, he said, is the real secret of success in all confidence tricks, three card tricks, and other frauds. For instance, in the three card trick, the cards are thrown down, and the dupe is to pick out the Jack to win. While the manipulator of the cards inadvertently but foolishly turns his back for a moment to see what the row behind him is about, a confederate quickly turns up the edge of a card displaying to 82 A CHAPLAIN ON DARTMOOR the eyes of the dupe the Jack. Having thus seen the card, he is ready to bet on finding it, thus feeling sure that he will win from the trickster, but when the bet is laid and he turns up what he is sure is the Jack, lo and behold he has selected the wrong card. He may be allowed for a time to win until he has been induced thereby to double or treble his stake, but the end is always the same, the biter bit, the deluded dupe duped, the man who believed he was sure to win despoiled of all he possessed.

Now the Americans pride themselves on being as cute as most people, and accordingly our friends set to work to exploit this little trait in their character. They opened a Money Lending and Insurance Office in New Yard and advertised largely in many provincial papers that they were prepared to lend certain sums of money on good security at a very moderate rate of interest. Soon applications came pouring in by every post. After some correspondence and a small fee paid to cover expenses, an agent is despatched to interview the borrower, and enquire as to the security that can be offered for the loan. The agent is, of course, one of the K. s, and he proceeds to some farmer, who has applied for a loan, offering good security for the loan, say, of 1,000. On arriving at the farm he meets a bright, engaging man who turns out to be the borrower, and they proceed to discuss the terms. There is first a small fee for preliminary expenses, and then the farmer must insure and pay the first premium for the policy. This the farmer does on the spot in ready money. " Now," says the agent, " what is the security you offer?: The mortgage-on my freehold farm and stock." Well, let me have a look round, as that is why my firm have sent me, as they can't lend a thousand pounds without good security."

On looking over the place the agent sees that the whole bag of tricks isn't worth anything like 1,000, and points this out, saying to the farmer: " It won't do–he is sure his firm would not entertain the matter for a moment. " Let us go into the house, and I will give you back the fees, and well consider the deal closed. I'm sorry; but business is business, you know, and unless you will accept a smaller sum that would be covered by the security, I can't advise my firm to loan such a sum as you have applied for." But the farmer wants his thousand, and by fair means or foul he means to have it. He entertains 84 A CHAPLAIN ON DARTMOOR the agent with food and drink– especially the latter, which seems to put K. on a friendly confidential footing, and over a pipe and another glass, the farmer comes to the point, and blurts out: " I suppose the decision of the firm depends entirely upon your report? " " Entirely," says the agent. Well, now, couldn't you make it in my favour if I make it worth your while?

" " I could, of course; but that depends upon what you mean, and if I can trust you not to give me away, as of course I should lose my job if it was known that I had taken a bribe to say your security for the loan was more than enough." " Well," says the farmer, "Ill give you my word not to say anything, and Ill give you a hundred pounds if you will make a satisfactory report as to the security. Ill give it you now, if youll write that report and let me post it." So the money is paid by the dishonest farmer, who is now certain in his own mind of getting that thousand pounds out of the Loan Office on security not worth half the money. He must have been much disappointed when he found in course of time that, instead of doing that very obliging firm, he had been done himself to the tune of a hundred pounds and a few extras, as of course he never heard anything more from them.

K. told me that they had hundreds of such cases, all very similar, but in some cases for large amounts, and consequently larger bribes.

They cleared out of New York before it got too hot for them, and, returning to England, were arrested for the turf frauds, and at last arrived at Dartmoor, where they found their confederate and chief had preceded them. This becoming known, they were shortly afterwards transferred to some other prison, and I don't know what became of them. B., their chief, was in course of time released, but getting into some fresh scrape was imprisoned in Belgium, and is said to have thrown himself over the top landing in the prison, and so killed himself. I have my own suspicion that he got this account inserted into the papers himself, when liberated, as it would certainly be to his advantage to be known as dead rather than alive! He was a clever rascal and quite equal to such an imposition.

In 1878, at Portland Prison, one morning I said good-bye to another notable prisoner, but of quite a different type to the foregoing ones.

He was of a fine, benevolent, and gentlemanly appearance, and we were quite sorry to lose him, as for some years past he had been an orderly or attendant in the prison infirmary, where he had been found most trustworthy and useful in ministering to the sick and dying. This man was the notorious forger of his father's will, by which he became the possessor of a large property valued at 200,000, and which was only resigned to the real owner, his younger brother, by his own confession and surrender. In his younger days he had always been treated by his father as the future heir, and had had committed to him the various duties connected with the management of the large property, so that on his father's death no suspicion attached to the forged will which put him in possession as owner. He was elected member of Parliament for Lambeth, and I think became an Under-Secretary of State. I first made his acquaintance in the hospital, and after some conversation he asked me if I should like to see his garden? As this was rather an unusual invitation in prison, on the part of a prisoner, I replied that I should very much like to see it, as I was very fond of flowers. He took me just over the other side of the hospital yard to what had once been the quarry from which the stone had been taken for the building of the hospital, and which at the first view appeared very much like any other large stone quarry. As we mounted some steps, I soon perceived that although it was a quarry, it was different to any other I had ever seen. On reaching a second terrace I found that like the first it was more like an ornamental garden than anything else; it was a mass of flowers in full bloom, and of all kinds. We sat down on a comfortable bench, and he told me its history. When he was appointed to the post of hospital orderly, some years back, he asked, as a favour, if he might work in this quarry and turn it into a garden, instead of exercising with the other men, as they walked round the yard every day for an hour or two's exercise. As the quarry was always in sight of the warders in the yard, and he was such a well-conducted prisoner, this request was granted, and had given him the greatest pleasure, so that he regarded the hours spent in the quarry as the happiest he had spent in prison. "But 5 I said, "how did you manage to get all these flowers; you can't go out to the shops and buy seeds, and I suppose 88 A CHAPLAIN ON DARTMOOK the seedsmen don't send you in their annual catalogues? " " No," he said, "I had some difficulties to get over when I first started; but that I got over them you see by the result. First I had to do a bit of quarrying, and then get soil into place to form these beds that you see. When they were ready it was about time to think of the plants, as spring was coming on. A few I obtained from the gardener who looks after the flower beds in the prison, and others were given me by friends interested in my experiment. For instance, you see all those pots of sweet brier and others of the same in those beds, all came from a small beginning. One day the assistant surgeon came into the hospital with a small bouquet in his button hole, and while he was giving me some instructions regarding a man who was seriously ill, I noticed that among the flowers in his button hole there was a small twig of sweet brier with just one seed pod on it, so I said: Would you be annoyed if I asked you a favour, sir? Not at all, he replied; what is it? 'Will you give me that bit of sweet brier that you have there? ' Why, of course I will, he said; you may have the lot– and he pulled out the bunch and tossed it to me. I found that there was also another treasure–a small slip of lavender. It is from those two I have reared all these sweet briers and lavenders that you see, and if you will accept one I shall be proud to give it you." I gladly accepted, and took home a pot containing a fine healthy shrub.

" After a time," he continued, "I got help from one or other of the officials in the shape of a packet of seeds, so that what was once a barren unsightly quarry now blossoms with roses, mignonette, asters, geraniums, and other flowers. It is one of the sights of the prison, and much admired by visitors."

While we were talking I noticed some sparrows hopping about in front of us, which appeared very tame, and I called his attention to them. " Oh, yes," he said, " they are friends of mine, and often cheer me up in my captivity. Now, they don't know you, and are a little shy; but if you will go to the end of the walk, and sit on that other seat, I will show you something." No sooner had I removed myself than the sparrows flew and hopped up to him, and perched on his shoulders and head, and fluttered about him without a trace of fear. He told me that 90 A CHAPLAIN ON DARTMOOR that also began in a small way. He took some crumbs out every day, and fed one hen sparrow, which in time became quite tame, and would come every day and perch quite close to him; but one day she failed to appear, and as this happened day after day he gave her up for lost, and had quite made up his mind that some evil had happened to her. " You see," he said, "I was only here for an hour or two at stated times, and if she came, as I daresay she did at other times, she would not find me, and may have concluded that something had happened to me, as I thought had happened to her. Well, I had quite given her up, and was trying to find another to take her place, when one afternoon, a month or six weeks after her disappearance, I was sitting here enjoying a little rest, when to my surprise I heard a familiar twitter, and soon after she came fluttering down and perched herself on the arm of the bench upon which I was sitting. I was, of course, delighted at her re-appearance, but as she kept on chirping I wondered what was the matter, but was not left long in doubt, for there on the path in front of me were seven well-grown youngsters, with the old mother as proud and fussy as much as to say, You see what I have been about–isn't that a family to be proud of? And, pointing to those around us, he said: There they are, with a few descendants, and all as tame as their mother."

"Well, now," I said, "tell me about your case; how was it that you got your long sentence? " He told me that he was conscience-stricken, and determined, as far as possible, to undo the wrong by confessing that he had forged his father's will, and so deprived his brother of his inheritance. I agreed with him that it was the best thing to do; but I said, "I hope, if I had been in your place, I should have had the moral courage to do as you did; but I would have done it without getting penal servitude for it." " So I did," he said, " at the first. When I made my first confession I was in Spain, where there is no extradition treaty; but it was explained to me that things could not be rectified unless I came back to England and signed a lot of documents and deeds of conveyance. If no exact promise was made to me, it was certainly implied that if I returned I should not be molested; but as soon as I set foot on land, at Dover, I was arrested, and here I am, with a 92 A CHAPLAIN ON DAETMOOR life sentence, but which I hope will soon be ended."

He was not disappointed, as in 1878 the order came for his release, and he returned home to live with his mother and sister, and spent the rest of his life in his favourite pursuit of gardening, raising grapes and other fruit for the market, and living down his past by a consistent and useful life. Here is an extract from the daily papers: rt There died at his residence, yesterday " afternoon, a hale old man of 80 who, until " advancing years restricted his activities, was " very well known to all his neighbours. For " five and twenty years he had lived here, and f being kindly and benevolently disposed, and " possessing some means, he was generally held " in high esteem."

He was a man of the most extraordinary moral courage. Instead of hiding himself under an alias in a strange town, he came back from prison to his old home, and began a new life, in which he made ample amends for his faults. He acquired the lease of a small plot of ground, and made a livelihood by cultivating it and selling the produce locally. His great speciality was the growing of hot-house grapes. He lived, after his sister's death, in a small cottage, in the simplest style, never drank or smoked, and, although he had little monej, was always ready to help those in straits if he could. He visited the sick, and had a Boys' Bible Class, and if he discovered a promising youth he watched over him, and did all that was possible to keep him in the right way and promote his temporal and spiritual welfare. Whatever faults he had in his earlier days, he showed in many ways that of him the saying was exemplified, "There shall be light at eventide."

Copied from a letter written by J. C. to his father:–

Think gently of the erring;

And do not thou forget, However darkly stained by sin,

He is thy brother yet– Heir of the self-same heritage, Child of the self-same God; He has but stumbled in the path Thou hast in weakness trod" Whenever I heard from their own lips the experiences of my brother chaplains on the scaffold when murderers were hanged. I could not be sufficiently thankful that although we had more than our share of murderers, we had no hangings 94 A CHAPLAIN ON DAKTMOOR at Dartmoor. Their sentences had been commuted to long terms of imprisonment or penal servitude for life, although this does not banish all hope, terrible as the sentence sounds. Their cases are always carefully considered, with a view to release after a certain number of years, and in many cases the men have at long last regained their freedom.

The chaplain of Exeter prison, whom I once had the pleasure of meeting on the Moor casually, and persuaded to come home and stay a day or two with me, and preach to the convicts on Sunday, gave me an account of his harrowing experience on the scaffold with Lee, the man who was convicted for the murder of his mistress at Babbacombe, and who escaped death by hanging by what can only be described as a miracle. As a full account of this has been given in the chaplain's recent publication called " From a Prison Cell," I will not repeat it here, but advise my readers to get the very interesting description of life in prison and read it for themselves. The man was brought to the execution shed in the usual way, accompanied by the chaplain and governor, executioner, and other officials, and placed on the drop. At the conclusion of the burial service the bolt was pulled, and the prisoner ought to have disappeared if the machinery was in order; but nothing happened, and the prisoner was removed, and the apparatus examined. When tested, it worked all right, and the drop fell as the bolt was pulled. Again the unfortunate man was placed on the death trap, and again it failed to work. Three times this was done with a like result, and the chaplain, without whose presence the execution could not be carried out, refused to stay any longer, and protested against any further torture of the unfortunate man. Accordingly he was taken back to his cell, and the Home Secretary granted a reprieve and commuted the sentence to penal servitude for life; but here is the extraordinary part of the business, that Lee himself declared that they would not be able to hang him, for that night he had had a dream foreshadowing what had just taken place, and he said that he had told this dream to a warder at six o'clock that morning– i. e., before the time when he would hear " the bell strike eight but not the clock strike nine." It was all very mysterious, but I could never find out whether it was true that he had told his dream before or only after the 96 A CHAPLAIN ON DARTMOOR failure to hang him. He lived to finish a long sentence and be liberated. He died at last in Australia, and always protested that he was innocent of the murder, and that his wonderful deliverance was proof positive of the fact.

That mistakes are sometimes made by juries the following incident, which was narrated to me by the man himself, is proof sufficient, if the man's word is to be believed, and he had not the slightest reason for deception.

Hearing that he was to be removed and taken next day to London, I went as usual to see him for a parting interview. I asked him if he knew why he was going before he had finished his sentence. Yes," he said, "I am going to give evidence against a soldier who murdered my wife last year, and nearly got me hanged for it. I daresay you have heard of the Lime Street murder; well, sir, that was the murder of which I was accused, arid for which I was nearly hanged. At the time it happened I was luckily shut up in Cardiff prison. One day I was told that I was wanted in London for a serious crime, and on the way up, in the train, I asked the governor if he would tell me the charge. No, I can tell you nothing he said; (you will hear soon enough. I asked, Is it very seiious? and thought over a good many of my past adventures, wondering which it could be that they had found out since my imprisonment. Arrived in London, in a few days time I found myself in court and to my surprise I was charged with the crime of murder–murdering my wife. Till then I did not know she was dead."

The details, as given by the prosecuting counsel, were that one evening his wife and a soldier went into one of the bars at a public-house, and were there by themselves drinking, when a scream from the woman brought the landlord and his niece on the scene. They found the woman stabbed to the heart arid dead, and the soldier with a slight wound in the chest. He declared that the woman's husband came in on them unexpectedly and inflicted the injuries on them before they could do anything to defend themselves. Now for the evidence. The proprietor said he saw a man just previous to the attack looking through the window from outside, and to the best of his belief the prisoner was that man, but he would not swear to him. The niece, with more confidence, said she saw him near the door, and could swear it was the 98 A CHAPLAIN ON DARTMOOR prisoner. He told me that he began to think that things were looking rather black, but knowing he was innocent, he had no fear of the result. A still greater surprise awaited him: his two sisters appeared as witnesses for the prosecution, and both testified that on that afternoon they saw their brother pass down the street, and remarked, Why, there's Bill; if he comes across his wife flirting about with that soldier, therell be murder done! " They were both quite positive that the man they saw was their brother Bill. These and some other witnesses were called. Amongst them the doctor, who said the woman was dead when he first saw her, but the soldier was only slightly injured, and was detained in hospital, but after having his wounds dressed was sent home.

The man told me the next thing he remembers was finding himself in the condemned cell under sentence of death for the murder of his wife. "After I had rallied and realised the seriousness of my position," he continued, "I asked the attendant warders if they could tell me the date of my wife's murder? Well, sir, you know what warders are, and how they would say, Well, Bill, if you don't know, I am sure we don't. When the governor came to see me on his daily round, I asked him the same question and implored him to tell me. All he would say was, My good man, you have only a short time to live; don't worry about such a detail; you have more serious matters to attend to. Listen to the chaplain, and do what he tells you? After a time, and by daily persistence, I got him to say, I do not see why I should not tell you, although you of all people must know. It was such and such a date (say, August 24th). But I was safe in Cardiff prison on that date, doing a sentence of eighteen months' imprisonment! ' Why did you not say so at the trial? he exclaimed. Because I wasn't asked, nor allowed to say anything." The result was that the sentence was quashed and the man sent back to Cardiff. He was in Dartmoor, when I knew him, for a fresh crime. The soldier was put on trial, and confessed that he it was who stabbed the woman, and afterwards himself, to give colour to his assertion that the husband had attacked them both. I believe he was let off with a very lenient sentence.

There may be some discrepancies in the above details, but the main facts are as stated, for I looked them up in the newspapers in what was called " The Limehouse Murder."

CHAPTER V.

DISCHARGES–HOSPITAL–CHAPEL SERVICES

ONE often meets with men who are doing their utmost to gain full marks and regain their liberty, and many who make no secret of their intention to escape at the first opportunity. I always impress upon the latter how much better it would be for them in the end if they would give up the folly of attempting an impossibility at the risk of their lives, and so spend their time in prison in reforming their characters, so that, once out, they would remain out as useful members of the commonwealth, instead of being a nuisance and expense as prisoners. " For," I ask, " if you were all let out to-morrow, or made your escape, how many of you would be back again within three months?: It was usual for me to interview each man on the eve of his discharge, when I did my best to impress upon him the desirability of turning over a new leaf and working for an honest living, and one's advice was always taken in good part, and promises made to lay it to heart. How often have I heard the words, "Ive had enough of this; I don't mean to come back "; although a favourite sarcastic retort was, "What's to become of you gentlemen if we don't any of us do so? " I was therefore rather taken aback, on going to the cells one evening to say good-bye to a well-conducted prisoner who was to be set at liberty next morning, when in answer to my advice he exclaimed, "But I don't want to go out. I have just told the governor so, and asked him not to discharge me." " Oh, come," I said, " there must be something wrong in the state of Denmark when a prisoner wants to stay in prison." Well," he replied, "I mean what I say. Why, look at it all round, and you will see how much better it is for me to be here than outside. Here I have good work to do, and I do it to the master tailor's satisfaction, and I don't know what Mr. Preston will do without me. I'm the cutter-out, you know, sir. I have a comfortable bed in a warm cell; I have as much food as I want, and warm clothes; and two doctors to attend me if I am taken ill.

102 A CHAPLAIN ON DARTMOOR

No! I don't want to leave, and I shall be much obliged if you will intercede for me with the governor, to keep me here. I dread what I shall have to face if I am discharged. No work– for who will employ me? No home, no money, no friends; what can I do but starve or steal, and that will be my fate. I dread it."

The following was found written on the walls of a prison, evidently by a man of somewhat the same opinion as my friend above:– I cannot take my walks abroad– I'm under lock and key; And much the public I applaud

For all their care of me.

Not more than others I deserve, In fact, much less than more; Yet I have food while others starve,

Or beg from door to door.

The lowest pauper in the street,

Half naked, I behold, While I am clad, from head to feet,

And covered from the cold.

Thousands there are who scarce can tell Where they may lay their head,

But Ive a warm and well-aired cell, A bath, good books, and bed.

While they are fed on workhouse fare,

And grudged their scanty food, Three times a day my meals I get, Sufficient, wholesome, good.

Then to the British public–" health "–

Who all our cares relieve; And when they treat us as they do

Theyll never want for thieves.

All depends upon where you are and how you regard your surroundings, for evidently the poet who composed the following, which I copied from his slate, had not the high opinion of some of the prisons that my previous friends had, and Dartmoor does not rank as prime favourite amongst the prisons whose inmate our poet has been at various times. It is a petition addressed to the Home Secretary (a privilege allowed once every six months to all who do not forfeit it by misconduct, and a delicate opportunity for blowing off steam and reminding chaplains and other officials of any little failures they have shown, the writer knowing that these officials must read whatever he chooses to write):

Right honourable sir, I humble beg

That you will listen to my woe, For what I suffer in Dartmoor,

The one half you do not know; From repeated attacks of this frightful disease I'm getting worse each day, So I humbly beg youll have me removed

Without the lest delay. In making my request in poetry, sir, I hope you won't think I'm joking, 104 A CHAPLAIN ON DARTMOOR

For the greatest favour you can bestow Is to send me back to Woking; For in this damp and foggy place It's impossible ever to get better, So I humbly trust, in addition to this,

You will grant me a special letter, As it would cause a deal of talk

All round, and in the prison– I mean if Niblo C. should be sent

Upon the public works. Why it would cause a deal more noise

Than the dispute between Kussians and Turks. In foggy weather, with my disease, Its impossible to last one hour, And if you doubt the accuracy of what I say, I refer you to Dr. Power, Or to any naval doctor,

Or one from the Plymouth garrison– They one and all would say the same,

And likewise Dr. Harrison. Since my reception in Dartmoor prison Ive been an unfortunate man, And I will tell you the why and the wherefore

As well as I possibly can: Well, every time Ive been in hospital– Its the whole truth what I say– For my medical treatment, I assure you, sir, Ive dearly had to pay. So I humbly beg, right honourable sir,

You will grant this humble petition, For I am sorry to say I have nothing to lose,

Having lost both health and commission. Such behaviour to poor sick men Is far from being just and right– And to report " sick " patients in hospital Is the officers' chief delight;

And perhaps, kind Sir, you might imagine that
They only do this to a dodger, But its done to all–George Bedwell
As well as poor Sir Koger. Like savage lions in this infirmary
The officers about are walking, To catch and report a dying poor man
For the frivolous charge of talking. And when we go out from hospital,
Our poor bodies they try to slaughter, By taking our reports, one at a time,
For which we get bread and water; For its such cruel treatment that's made me what I am,
And brought me near the grave. So in conclusion, right honourable sir,
My removal I humbly crave.

It is pleasing to record that the petition was granted, and shortly afterwards the poet was removed to Woking, where we will hope he found his hospital treatment more to his liking.

Here is another effusion written by a prisoner whose description of his surroundings is poetical, if written in prose, and does credit to his powers of observation. I do not think it was written with a view of currying favour with the authorities, who, he knew, would read it:–

Dear Parents, 24th A P ril 1896 I am quite well and comfortable– i. e., as comfortable as circumstances will permit. Tis very pleasant here at present–a constant 106 A CHAPLAIN ON DARTMOOR succession of hills and valleys, little brooks and fields–some green, others covered with heather–stretching in the far distance to the sky line, ever changing in the sun's rays, cattle grazing, young lambs playing, which is a very soothing and charming sight to us.

We are up at 5 a. m., to breakfast by 6-30; church at 7; going to work at 7-30. We have good distances to go sometimes. We get back to dinner by 11-15 (am writing now), off out again by 1 p. m., then in by 5 p. m.; supper; then to bed by 8 p. m. So that you see I have plenty of fresh air and good food– plenty, but of course of a coarse nature. Mine is all field work at present, but I have got permission to learn a trade, and I have chosen shoemaking. I shall be starting presently.

There are objects of interest about here– monuments to the French prisoners of war; inscriptions in French over old gateways, on walls and other places, fine specimens of granite spar, variegated stone, Druidical relics in pillars, etc. Next time I write it will be six months, unless I can get special permission from the Governor. As I am having no visits I may succeed.

The Governor is all that can be desired in a place like this, as well as the officers. They all have a great deal to put up with, as well as we. So keeping that in mind they are all right. Now you will know how I am situated here. I thought that you would like to know all that you could, etc., etc.

I have all your letters now, even your first.

I often read them on Sunday afternoons.

The following shows that some of the prisoners have a studious turn of mind, and I have often been surprised at the progress some men have made in languages, especially in French, Latin, and Greek. There was always a great demand for dictionaries, especially French, no doubt with a view to transferring their operations to French soil on their release.

I still study very earnestly. As soon as it is light in the morning, I sit up in bed, and read a page or two of Pliny, Sallust, or Horace, in Latin. For half an hour after breakfast I study German, and again from 6-30 p. m. to 7-45 for three-quarters of an hour; at midday I transcribe Latin. For about an hour after supper I translate English into French and vice versa. After going to bed I read some 108 A CHAPLAIN ON DARTMOOR

French book until it becomes too dark to see. Then I lie down and turn some of the lines of Horace into English verse, or oftener, as you will learn, sit up and do it. I don't read very much in English, and then only historical or scientific works. Sallust's Catalina and Jugurthenum and the Satires of Horace I have well digested, the second Epodus of the latter I have turned into English verse, etc., etc.

Jan. 8th, 1897.

The doctor had granted me more food, and in consequence I felt better than formerly, and I have no doubt that my health wo aid have gone on improving if it had been continued to me, but having allowed me to tell you that it had been granted, he then took it from me. There is more suffering in prison from hunger than from anything else. Three men made their escape the day before Christmas. One was shot dead, another wounded, the third– after being chased for three days by two-legged bloodhounds–was captured and brought back. All of them had become desperate from hunger, and not liking to die without a struggle, they thought they would have a run for it. The one they killed is the best off. If I could make sure of being shot dead, as he was, I too would make a bolt for liberty.

A letter from S. W. to his wife:– I often think of your cottage That stands in John Street– If its outside is humble, Its inside is neat.

I love my sweet Jane,

She's buxom and fair, And she sings like a birdie

To welcome me there.

So I mind not the hardships

Nor trouble of life, For we keep up the courtship

Although she's my wife.

EXTRACTS FROM DIARY. February 1st, 1877.

A Prussian here told me the following about a fellow countryman of his now in the prison. He is here for stealing a lot of valuables from a nobleman's house, amongst them being an iron chest about 2 feet long. He was offered by the prosecutor that he would withdraw from the charge, give him 500, and send him to America, if he would restore the iron safe with its contents. The man says he has buried it not far 110 A CHAPLAIN ON DARTMOOR from the nobleman's house, and his friend has told him the exact place, and how to find it. He wants me to move in the matter, thinking if it could be restored something might be done to reduce their sentence. Told him he had better apply to the Governor.

February, 1877.

Saw a man to-day taking exercise in the yard. He made progress between jumping and swimming. He is thought by the doctors to be shamming. He declares his leg is withering. There are several similar cases, but generally they overdo the performance. The Governor tells me of a man who went doubled up and quite deformed for more than a year, but suddenly, in his office, stood upright, and stretching himself exclaimed, "Well, Ive had enough of that!"

Amongst the men I interviewed to-day three cried, or rather blubbered, like big schoolboys. The subjects discussed were certainly painful and affecting, and I do not think they were sham tears, but certainly the tears were there, and visible to the naked eye. I wonder if any other clergyman in the land has had a similar experience to-day–three grown-up men weeping!

HOSPITAL.

The hospital is a large building containing a large open ward, with adjoining dispensary, and three other long corridor wards, with separate cells on either side. Everything spick and span, as a hospital should be. In each of these wards prayers were read every morning by the chaplain and scripture reader, each prisoner being afterwards visited and talked with. In the long corridors my desk was placed in the middle of the passage, about halfway down, and the men who were out of bed stood each at his door, which was opened for the purpose. For the most part the behaviour was exemplary, and although occasionally a loaf of brown bread was seen to whizz across from one side to the other, on the whole there was nothing to complain of. Occasionally one's nerves were tried by an unexpected incident. I was one morning kneeling at my prayer desk, in the middle of the passage, when a man in his night-shirt appeared at the far end of the passage, and came with a hop, skip, and a jump straight down the passage, which my prayer desk almost blocked. I saw him coming, and expected that he would bowl me over on his mad rush. There was no 112 A CHAPLAIN ON DARTMOOR time to get up off my knees, so I just braced myself to receive the shock and went on with the prayers. When he reached the desk, however, instead of knocking it over, he very carefully sidled past, and continued his wild career to the end of the passage, when he collapsed in a heap, and appeared to be in a fit, foaming at the mouth and struggling in convulsions. His consideration for me and my desk was to his own undoing, for the doctor asked me, later on, whether he got past the obstruction without upsetting me. I said, "Yes, he did; much to my relief." " Well, that settles it," said the doctor, "if it had been genuine epilepsy, he would have sent you and your desk flying." It turned out that the doctor was right– the man was shamming a fit. To prevent this malingering, every care is taken to hide any genuine fit from the eyes of other prisoners, lest they should be able to imitate what they have seen.

The doctor kindly allowed me, in serious cases, to bring in any little luxury the man might be craving for, and sometimes requests were made to one which it was difficult to execute. Of course anything necessary in the way of diet the doctor could order, and it would be supplied, so that my permission only applied to some occasional trifle, such as a few strawberries or grapes in their season. I remember a man asking me if I would bring him a few grapes. At the time I was able to get him some hothouse black grapes, but, later on, he asked me again, and then I could only get the common white Spanish ones, which are not to be compared with the others. As these were the only ones procurable, I took them in and gave them to him in a paper bag. Next morning he handed me back the empty bag and informed me that those white grapes were rubbish, and the doctor said he was to have black Hamburg. " But what have you done with the rubbish? " I said. " Oh, Ive eaten them." " Good man," I replied," you won't get any more for some time." About the most difficult request for me to fulfil was in the case of a dying man, to whom I said, "You don't seem to be taking your food. Is there anything you fancy that I can get you? " "Well, sir," he said, "it's a simple and perhaps curious request, but of all things I can think of, I should like a drink of water from that cold spring in your yard!?: " All 114 A CHAPLAIN ON DARTMOOR right," I said, "Ill get it for you." I took an empty wine bottle at home, filled it from the spring in the yard, and took it up to the prison.

Now, to enter the prison, one has to pass through the two big entrance gates, which can only be opened and shut by the gatekeeper, who is responsible for everybody and everything that goes in or out at the gate. How would he regard my bottle of water? When I produced it, and told him I had the doctor's permission to give it to a sick prisoner, he looked a little doubtful, so I said, "Here, take it, and taste it, if you don't believe me." " Oh, all right, sir," he said, " of course I take your word for it." " Now H.," I said, " could you prevent me if I refused any explanation, or suppose I had that bottle in my pocket, could you claim any right to search me? J " No," he said, "I have no right to search a superior officer, but this is what I could and should do if I had any suspicion, I should refuse to open that gate and let you in until I had sent for the governor to see you."

So I and my bottle were admitted and the dying man's thirst was quenched. Much ado about nothing, as it was precisely the same water that was supplied to the Hospital. It was a sick man's fancy, quickened perhaps by the remembrance of a draught from my spring on some hot thirsty day when at work there.

CHAPLAINS.

In magazine articles and books written by prisoners after their discharge, the prison chaplain is very often unfairly pictured and misrepresented, although I have read some descriptions by the latter not at all unfavourable, and sometimes flattering. At first sight the post of prison chaplain is by no means attractive, and as I have said in another place, it was to my mind the most repulsive duty that I could conceive, and when the offer was first made to me and I was discussing with a brother curate, whose opinion on most subjects I valued highly, his remark was, "Don't take it; I am sure you won't like it; why, you will have to keep a diary! " " Well, I don't see much harm in that." He replied, "It implies supervision and restrictions; you won't like it." I am glad that his advice was not followed, and I never regretted my acceptance of the post, as I found it, contrary to my expectations, 116 A CHAPLAIN ON DAETMOOR both interesting and stimulating. And after all the years I have spent in prison and now that I am laid on the shelf, I would willingly go back if it were permissible. It is, I think, in " Adam Bede," when the heroine is in prison and her friends are discussing the advisability of sending into the prison their own favourite clergyman to minister to her, that one makes the remark, "I think the prison chaplains are taken from the fag-end of the clergy." On another occasion two of his flock in a country town are discussing the resignation of their curate to take up his appointment to a prison as chaplain, and one of them remarked, "What a success he would be if he only emptied the prison as he had emptied their Church by his preaching! " But then country farmers are not good judges in matters pertaining to the Church. In a certain large county town the Bishop was holding a Visitation, when all his clergy in that Deanery are cited to attend. A farmer, noticing the large number of clergymen in the streets, asked his friend the reason. " Oh," he replied, " it is the triennial Visitation." " What's that?" said the other. Why, every three years all the clergy meet to exchange sermons." "Well,"

said his friend, " our Vicar always gets the worst over the deal, for his sermons get duller and duller." This is about as truthful as the other yarns so frequent in the quotations I have given above.

The greatest care is, I believe, taken by the authorities in the selection of suitable men from the large number of candidates always on the list of applicants, and so far as I have had experience of them, they have always appeared to be hard-working conscientious men, and at the same time sympathetic and kindly disposed, ready to do all in their power to alleviate the hard lot of their flock. Of course to a certain extent they are handicapped by restrictions and prison rules, and are on their honour strictly to keep the rules and maintain discipline. This at times makes their task a delicate and difficult one. For instance a man in great trouble appeals to me to write a letter to his wife, as she is in a dangerous and delicate position. If I will send her a word from him it may be the means of saving her from serious danger. It seems hard to refuse, and all I can promise is that if he will get the governor's permission for me to do this I will gladly do so, 118 A CHAPLAIN ON DARTMOOR but not otherwise. It seems rather a hard case and sounds so plausible that many a locum tenens officiating during my absence has been enticed to break the rules of the prison out of pity for the man and his wife; but once you do so, you are in the man's power, and he will use it by pressing other requests and threaten to expose you for having written to his wife. This was once brought home forcibly to me by an instance which personally concerned me. We had a most troublesome prisoner, who seemed quite irreclaimable, and often as I tried my best to tame him I was always met with failure, but in conversation I found out from him that there was a good lady outside who had taken an interest in him, and as far as I could gather was the only person who had influenced him for good, and so I suggested that he should write to her, and I was sure she would write a nice letter in return. No, he wouldn't write. " Well shall I write to her and tell her you would like to hear from her? " He jumped at this, and said how glad he would be if I would do so. Accordingly I wrote and told her that I thought a letter from her might do good, as she seemed to have had an influence over him, and this was sorely needed now as he was very hard and unmanageable. I took this to the governor and asked him if he would initial it, so that I might send it, as of course without his permission I could not do so. In due time a very nice answer from the lady was received, which in the same way I took to the governor and asked him to pass it, which he did by putting his initials in the corner. I took it to the prisoner, who flew into a violent temper, and declared that if he had known the letters were to pass through the governor's hands he would not have consented to my writing on his behalf. Of course I saw then why he so readily accepted my offer. He thought if I broke the rules by writing without the governor's knowledge I should be in his power, I don't say that all the prisoners would be such sneaks, but it was always safest to be on one's guard in such matters.

The duties of a chaplain as laid down by the Secretary of State in the Rules for the Government of Prisons are at once arduous and delicate. He is required to visit the prison daily, to conduct the Sunday and week-day services, to take charge of the library, to see all prisoners 120 A CHAPLAIN ON DARTMOOR on reception and discharge, and as often as possible to visit the men in their cells. The last is especially important, and is the best means of establishing friendly relations with the men. At mid-day, and in the evenings, when the prisoners are in their cells, he is free to go where he chooses. He has keys that will open any door of the prison or cell, and then with no other attendant he can have a chat with its inmate for as long as he chooses. The only drawback to this is that the time is limited, as of course the men are out at work for the greater part of the day, and it is only at the dinner hour and for a couple of hours in the evening that they are at home and accessible to their visitor. When I first went to Dartmoor I found that if a prisoner wanted to see the chaplain he had to give his name in to the warder, just as he did if he wanted an interview with the governor or doctor; but I soon found it necessary to alter this, as the men were discouraged by being questioned by the warder as to what they wanted to see the chaplain for, etc., so I had two wooden boxes with a slit at the top like a money box put at the entrance into chapel, and tin tallies stamped with the number of the cell and placed in every cell, so that any day, and every day if they liked, they could take the tallies to chapel, drop them into the box, and in due course the chaplain took them back to the cells and learned the men's requests. The only drawback to this was that there are always in every prison a certain number of prisoners who take delight in giving as much trouble as possible and will put down their names on every occasion for an interview with governor, doctor, or any other official. One got to know these men, and if their tallies appeared too often they were kept in hand for a time and the owner allowed to wait.

I adopted another plan to afford the men an opportunity for an interview. On Sundays after service in chapel the men had an hour's exercise in one of the largest yards. Here they walked round in single file in a wide circle, but no talking was allowed. I. usually joined them, and took my walk inside the circle of men, but walking in the opposite direction, and any prisoner who liked could step out of the circle and join me in my walk, whilst we conversed together. In time I found the men gladly availed themselves of this opening for a chat, 122 A CHAPLAIN ON DARTMOOR and for the hour I was never without a companion. At first they were very shy and hung back, not liking, I suppose, to be seen by the others in such friendly relations with the chaplain, but they soon got over this, and if I was left without a companion I had only to beckon to this one or that and he would instantly join me. I made many friends in this way, and if a prisoner complained that I did not visit him I could always reply, "If you wanted to have a visit why didn't you tell me so on Sunday afternoon in the yard?"

In visiting the different cells it was always necessary to remember that although you had a key that would open a cell door from the outside, you had no means of opening a cell door from within, as there was no keyhole, and unless you were careful to shoot the lock when you entered, it was very easy to close the door and the lock would snap to very easily, and you would find yourself locked in with the prisoner and no means of getting out until someone came with a key outside and unlocked the door and set you free. On several occasions through inadvertence this happened to me, and it was not at all a pleasant sensation to find oneself a prisoner locked in a cell, where one's imprisonment might last an hour or so, unless one could attract the attention of the one warder who was in sole charge of the large prison with its four or five landings to perambulate. I remember on one occasion having something of importance to communicate to a prisoner. On entering I gave the door a slight push, not intending to close it, but only partially to hide us from anyone passing the open door. As I did so I heard a click behind me and knew that the door had locked. The prisoner smiled and said, "Youve done it this time, and may have to stop until the warders come round at the end of the dinner hour and unlock all the doors." (Well," I said, " let us finish the business I came about and then we will see about getting out. I don't want to stop here till then as it is only about 12 o'clock." I then read the letter to him from his wife, which conveyed the announcement of his mother's death or something of the kind, " and now," I said, " shove your flag out."

This is a signal attached to every cell, which, when pushed out, informs the warder in the hall that the prisoner wants his cell door opened.

124 A CHAPLAIN ON DARTMOOR

He put out the signal and waited, but in vain. We could hear the footsteps of the officer in the distance, but he didn't seem to be coming any nearer, and getting tired of my company I began to kick at the door in hopes that that might attract the notice of the warder, but it didn't, and the prisoner advised me not to go on with it. " Why not? " I said, " he must hear it." " Yes," he said, " he will hear that, and a good deal more, because all the prisoners near us will join in and kick their doors." And sure enough they did, so that by the time the warder arrived there was a fine row going on on all sides, and it was some time before he discovered the flag outside and opened the door and set me free.

I always liked visiting the men in their cells where we could come face to face and have a straight talk with one another, and from the most of them one was always sure of a welcome if only because there was the opportunity to talk without fear of any ill consequences, the chaplain being about the only person in the prison to whom this privilege appertains. I have heard some queer tales as to undiscovered crimes, buried treasure, and false imprisonments, and although I must often have rubbed the men up on a sore place, any rudeness or rebuff was most unusual, and was invariably followed by some sort of apology. I hope the pleasure of my visits was mutual, and I have good reason to think it was, as for some time after my retirement I had many letters from the men and frequent requests that if possible I would pay them a visit. This I did with permission from the authorities, and spending a day on the moor I put in some hour or two visiting my old parishioners.

However many disappointments meet him to damp his ardour, how many hopes may be quenched, he never loses heart, but plods on from day to day, making the best of his opportunities as they crop up. Of course his work carries with it special responsibilities and anxieties, but he never allows this to become too overwhelming, but finds relief in a day on the moor with rod or gun, and returns to work with a lightened mind. Without some such relaxation it would be very hard to carry on, and in this respect I think Dartmoor Prison, with its surrounding moorland and sparkling rivers, is to be preferred to any other prison in the service.

126 A CHAPLAIN ON DARTMOOR

When it was known that I was about to retire the prisoners told me that they could only testify their appreciation of my services by writing me some very touching letters, but one or two went a step further than this. Hearing that the warders and a few friends were about to make me a substantial present as a parting memento of our long association, one old burglar, with a smile on his ugly old face, said to me just before I was leaving, "We have heard that the officers are going to present you with a piece of plate, and we wish we could do the same. Now, sir, if only you could persuade the governor to let me and my mate out for a night, and you could tell us where there is a nice piece of silver you would like, well, we would do the rest, and you should have it." I told him I would take the will for the deed, and thanked them all the same.

CHAPEL SERVICES.

One of the most remarkable and affecting sights in the whole routine of the day is the assembly in chapel every morning of all the convicts, about a thousand in number, with their attendant warders. Here in the front we see the full choir, about thirty in number, seated on three sides of a square round the harmonium, with the head schoolmaster as organist and choir master, whilst on forms, row upon row, stretching into the distance, are seated the men with warders, on raised seats, to keep a watch and see that there is no talking or misbehaviour. And here it may be recorded that few reports are made of misconduct in chapel. One exception comes to my mind at a confirmation. At the conclusion of the Bishop's address a cry was heard from the far end of the big chapel of " Vive Vanarchie; a bas le religion," and an Italian prisoner, convicted of the manufacture of bombs, was gently seized by the warders and lifted over the heads of the other men and deposited outside without interfering with the Bishop's encouraging words. When I afterwards visited the man and asked him for an explanation of his conduct, he assured me in his broken English that he had a good deal more he wanted to say but they did not give him time. " I was outside before I had time to finish." "Well," I said, "I heard what you did say, and also saw what happened to you, and it looked to me more like h bas Vanarclm and vive le religion, but don't do it 128 A CHAPLAIN ON DARTMOOR again, at any rate in church." The Bishop interceded for him and accordingly he was let off very lightly. He gave no further trouble, at any rate when in chapel.

Before proceeding to work all the men attend the service, which is held at 7 a. m. every morning, summer and winter alike, and a short service is read by the chaplain and a short address given. It is rather a trial to one's capacity as a preacher to be called upon at that time of day and limited to a few minutes to say anything very impressive; but I always hoped that a few straight words might catch and perhaps be thought over during the long day's monotony of work. At any rate it kept one in practice, and was of benefit to the preacher if not to the prisoners.

The congregation is certainly a mixed multitude. Here before us we have four or five doctors, some schoolmasters and clerks, journalists, and two clergymen, not both of the established church, and all quite capable of criticising the sermon, besides many murderers, thieves, pickpockets, receivers, and professors in crime. I once read a short article by a writer who attended one of our services on Sunday, and he said that to stand up and preach to such a congregation needed a man with nerves of iron. I did not know that I had this qualification, and felt that there was no need to be nervous if one was prepared to say anything worth listening to, and that I might say it the better I had the pulpit, which was high up in the roof, brought some feet lower so as to be on a level with the men, and able, in their midst, to speak almost face to face. I did not realise that there was any risk in this, until one day a man told me that he had his boot off to throw at my head because I was speaking of him and his doings in too personal a manner. I asked him where he was sitting, and when told only about three seats back from the pulpit, I asked him if he would mind going a little further back as the chance of his missing me would be greater.

This was a most exceptional case, and was, after all, only a threat, and the attention and behaviour of the men, when a good preacher is in the pulpit, is something extraordinary. And many such have been kind enough to respond to my invitation. I am afraid that many a hard-worked clergyman taking his holiday on 130 A CHAPLAIN ON DARTMOOR the moor must have deemed me an insufferable nuisance by my disturbance of his well-earned rest, in asking him to preach in the chapel next Sunday, a request that none had the heart to refuse. Amongst them were the late Bishop of Marlborough, the late Bishop Knight Bruce, the late Bishop of Wakefield (Walsham How), the Bishop of Exeter, Canon Cornish, Dr. Butler, and many other notable preachers. We also had a yearly visit for a ten days' mission by evangelists from the Church Army, whose stirring addresses greatly interested the men. Of course on returning from one's annual leave, when a substitute had been taking the duty, one had the usual backhanded compliment paid one: " Ah, sir! that was something like a preacher; we were saying how we wished. oh! I beg pardon, I forgot who I was speaking to. No offence, sir."

As to sermons. Those seemed to me to have the best effect which were plain and to the point–short, aptly illustrated, and not too decidedly divided into heads. One never knows how they will apply the illustrations, or anecdotes, so that it is better to make the application direct oneself. I remember on one occasion preaching on repentance, and the duty of owning up to one's faults, and not making matters worse by trying to cover the first sin by perhaps a worse, telling a lie to hide it. I illustrated this by an anecdote of a certain King of France who once visited one of the large prisons (Toulon. I think it was) and made a tour of the prison, interviewing any prisoner he met about the grounds. The first he met, to the King's enquiry: "What is your crime, my man?" replied that he was innocent and had committed no crime deserving such a punishment. That will do, you can go on with your work." Again and again he received a similar answer to the question, until, if they were to be believed, there was hardly a guilty man in the prison; but at last he came to a man who owned up to his guilt, and told the King he had only got what he deserved, for there was hardly a crime under the sun he had not committed, but he had one hope left, and that was in the King's mercy. (That is the man for my pardon," said the King, and ordered the man's release.

The week following, amongst the petitions to the Home Secretary I had to precis, there was one from a prisoner containing the substance 132 A CHAPLAIN ON DARTMOOR of my illustration, and saying that there was not a crime under the sun he had not committed, but cast himself on the mercy of the Home Secretary who, he had been told, was a merciful man: that was his hope. Some time later I was visiting a man in his cell who recalled the incident to my mind by asking me if on discharge one was liable to be re-arrested for some former crime other than that for which the penalty had been paid. Yes," I said, " undoubtedly; I have known men re-arrested on their release; but what's troubling you now, what have you done?"

" It isn't what Ive done, sir, but what Ive written."

Why of course, you wrote that petition some months ago and said there wasn't a crime under the sun you had not committed. You haven't committed murder have you, or bigamy?:

" Why no, but you know what you said in that sermon about the King of France, and I thought if I said the same the Home Secretary would do what the King did, but it is evident he is not so merciful."

" Perhaps not," I said, " but I don't think he will punish you for what you write, but only for what you have done."

The following was sent to me by a visitor who had attended the service one Sunday, as reflecting the memories of the service he had been privileged to join in:– I knelt within the house of prayer, This gleamy quiet day of rest, And felt myself a welcome guest,

Bidden, with more, a feast to share.

Before me, through the Eastern light, I saw the sweep of moorland hills, And felt the calm their strength instils,

The solace of their girdling might.

Below the table Christ has spread

The tokens of His dying love,

Unchanging as the hills above: The wine of life–the living bread.

On either side the mandates ten Blazed out in golden letters grand, In face of those whose lives depraved

Had shut them from their fellow men.

The grey-haired convict, and the boys Scarce grown to manhood, gathered there To join with us in praise and prayer,

To hear of pardon, life, and joys.

" Our Father " fell from lips of all;

" Forgive us," all of us did cry;

Those still far off and those brought nigh Together at God's footstool fall.

134 A CHAPLAIN ON DARTMOOR

The words of pardon and of peace To those who sorrow from the heart, Who feel the burden of the smart

And seek from Him who died–release.

Brave words of cheer the preacher spoke To the desponding souls, to rise And lift their dreary clouded eyes

To Him who breaks sin's strongest yoke.

We knelt again in prayer; again

The sense of oneness in our fall,

And needed mercy proffered all, Knit me to my brother men.

The parting blessing now is said: I rise and see the eternal hills, And know the eternal love that fills

His heart who their foundations laid.

There is nothing more trying to a chaplain at times, especially if he does not feel quite up to the mark on a Saturday morning, than to put together a few thoughts for his two Sunday sermons, and it is not made easier when week after week and year after year he has to address the same congregation. He knows that to keep their attention there is nothing more effectual than illustrations drawn from real life, the more modern the better, but he knows as well as the congregation do that news of the day is strictly verbolen.

I remember once preaching on the danger of under-estimating the power of the enemy, and that nothing could be more helpful to the great enemy than to deny his personality or his power: to persuade oneself that there is no such a person as Satan, or any power of evil to influence us, is to give a great advantage, and is contrary to everybody's experience of life. Everybody must see there is such design at work, speaking of a designer, unseen, but very powerful and cunning, who suits his temptation to each, according to his circumstances and weakness. For instance, I am never tempted to steal a watch, because already I have one; I am not tempted to commit murder, because I haven't an enemy in the world; but what I am tempted to do is just where I am weakest– the bad-tempered to quarrel, the impure to yield to his passion, etc., and I illustrated this by what I had just been reading in the papers about the tragedy in South Africa, when at Isandula the Welsh Regiment had been exterminated by hordes of Zulus, whom our commanders had under-estimated as to numbers and propinquity. Owing to this many lives had been lost, which would not have happened 136 A CHAPLAIN ON DARTMOOR had it been known that the enemy were so near. Take this into account," I said, " as you go through life, and remember you have enemies without as well as within you, and therefore take unto you the whole armour of God if you are to withstand the enemies in the evil day."

Next day I was called over the coals in a friendly way by the governor, who was present at the service. " Don't you know," he said, " that it's against the rules to tell the prisoners the news of the day? How about yesterday's sermon? " " Oh! well," I said, " it came pat to what I was preaching about, and couldn't do any harm." " Perhaps not," he said, " but how many applications do you think I have had for special letters, because the applicants have brothers or fathers in the Welsh Regiment and think they may be amongst the slain. How can I say no, when a man is weeping over a lost brother? Half the prison according to their own tale must have had relatives in that particular regiment, and didn't the chaplain tell them in his sermon they were all killed!"

I told the governor to tell them the following tale I had read somewhere in a newspaper, when they came next time with such a yarn:

Private OFlynn once went to his colonel, as these men did to the governor. The colonel was a strict disciplinarian, and when Private OFlynn made his request for two weeks' leave of absence, naturally the colonel asked him why he wanted it. Pat answered, "My wife is very sick and the children are not well, and if ye didn't mind she would like to have me home for a few weeks to give her a bit of assistance."

The colonel eyed him for a few minutes and said, "Pat, I might grant your request but I got a letter from your wife this morning saying that she didn't want you home;

that you were a nuisance and raised the devil whenever you were there. She hopes I won't grant you any more furloughs." " That settles it, I suppose I can't get the furlough then," said Pat.

" No, I'm afraid not, Patrick. It wouldn't be well for me to do so under the circumstances."

It was Patrick's turn now to eye the colonel, as he started for the door. Stopping suddenly he said, "Colonel, can I say something to you?"

" Certainly Pat, what is it? " You won't get mad, colonel, if I say it? J:

" Certainly not, what is it?"

138 A CHAPLAIN ON DARTMOOR

" I think there are two of us; I'm one; I was never married in me life."

But talking about news of the day, it is quite wonderful how it filters into a prison. The day after the boat race a man in the infirmary exclaimed, when I approached his bedside, "So Oxford won the race yesterday; " and at another time, a day or two after the event, another invalid greeted me with the news that old " Dizzy" was dead. How they learn of these events, and so soon, is one of the mysteries of prison life.

As to sermons in general, I always found that those illustrated by some tale of a passing event known to them kept their attention best. Perhaps the following one will best show the kind of sermon I mean. There was an annual sale of the surplus stock on the prison farm, when sheep, pigs, horses, and ponies are sold by auction, and good prices are made, as the stock is known to be of first-class quality, and attracts buyers from all parts of the county. So on the following Sunday I availed myself of it as affording a good illustration of the lesson I wanted to impress upon my flock. I begin by saying, I suppose we must have a text or they won't think it is a sermon, so we will take the words of St. James, III: We put bits in the horses' mouths and we turn about their whole body also."

St. James is here speaking of the tongue and the power for evil there is in our words, and that the speech of a man shows whether he can control himself when tempted to other sins than evil speaking. If he cannot refrain from swearing or bad language when there is no earthly gain to be got, how is he likely to refrain from worse sins when some worldly gain increases the temptation? Whoever heard of any man getting any good by swearing or using bad language? So St. James tells us the tongue is a little member but may do infinite harm, and therefore we ought to think before we speak, and keep careful watch over our tongue. Well, to show you what I mean," I continue,: t you know that the day before yesterday we had our annual sale of the prison stock, and amongst other animals some very nice horses were sold. I was present, and saw one fine horse trotted round the ring led by a prisoner who was his groom. Bids, beginning at 20, soon ran up to 50 and 60, and I think 140 A CHAPLAIN ON DARTMOOR he was sold at that price. Now I couldn't help thinking, if slavery were still allowed in this country, and the man were put up for sale, how much would he fetch? Would anyone give half as much for the man as for the horse? But why not? Surely a man is of more value than a horse, and if not, why not? St. James tells us in the words of my text, We put bits in the horses' mouths and turn about their whole bodies. If we can't do that we have no control over them and they are useless. They are not worth a penny. And so it is with men. If we can control them or, better still, if they have learned to control themselves, then they become of great value to themselves and to their fellow-men. In the case of the horse, a wild horse that we cannot bit is a nuisance and of no value. He runs wild and isn't worth his keep. So St. James says it is with ships: Though they are so great, and are driven by rough winds, yet are they turned about by a very small rudder. We know what happens if the rudder is broken or carried away: the ship is out of control and is wrecked on the rocks. So if we would not be without value, like a wild horse, or a danger to our fellow-men, like a rudderless ship to her passengers, we must be under control. We must practise by the help of God's good spirit self-control," etc., etc.

I have heard some very good sermons preached in the chapel, and if they were to the point and not too long, they were listened to with marked interest by the mixed congregation. No doubt many of the men were indifferent, but their seclusion and quiet in the cell was in favour of some after-thought on the subject they had been listening to, and if one touched their feelings or rubbed them up the wrong way one was pretty sure to hear of it during the following week.

They ought certainly to be good judges of a sermon, if that judgment is to be acquired by the number they have listened to. Twice every Sunday, year after year, was a tax on the preacher if not on the congregation, and the number of texts and sermons some of them must have listened to in the course of their prison life must have exceeded those of any other class of men in the same time. I wonder if, when free, they ever voluntarily attended a place of worship.

To be listened to patiently Sunday after 142 A CHAPLAIN ON DARTMOOK

Sunday one was bound to do one's best to be interesting, and to choose suitable texts and subjects, and although I had various useful hints given me by the more intelligent and well-conducted prisoners, I was only once or twice interrupted in my sermon by any outspoken remark.

Once when preaching about repentance-true repentance, what it is, and what it is not– I was saying that some mistakes are made by supposing that it is mere sorrow for sin, and I said if that were true we all repented sooner or later, because sorrow followed sin as certainly as night followed day; true repentance shows itself in a change of mind as regards our outlook upon sin. If I am on the road to Plymouth and change my mind, what do I do? It would be absurd to say I have changed my mind if I continue on the same course. No; but if I have repented or changed my mind, I turn back and retrace my steps. Then repentance if of the right kind shows itself in a change of conduct, as when the liar learns to speak the truth, the thief gives up his thieving, the ill-tempered learns to control his temper, the cruel learns to be kind and gentle, etc.

At this there was a loud explosion from the middle of the chapel. You should tell that to the governor; he's murdering me!" The governor happened to be present, but the man could not see him. I went quickly on as though nothing had happened, and there was no further interruption. Shortly afterwards I went to see the man in his cell, and asked him what he meant by his bad behaviour, and his only excuse was that he was being badly treated by the governor.

" But," I said, " you are not being badly treated by me, and it was too bad to interrupt me in my sermon; how would you like it if you were preaching to a lot of men and I were to shout out like you did?:

" Well," he said, "I didn't mean to bother you, and I won't do it again."

I replied: ' You won't at any rate for some time, as you won't be allowed to come to chapel until you have learned how to behave."

I always found that they very much disliked being kept in their cell instead of coming to chapel. It was not perhaps from any religious motive that they wanted to come, but the monotony of the cell was so irksome that they 144 A CHAPLAIN ON DARTMOOR preferred the chapel service with its singing and even its preaching to the solitary confinement and their own thoughts. I remember how one very intelligent man, who could speak several languages, and when at liberty had moved in the best society, appealed to me again and again to be allowed to attend the services on Sunday. He had entered himself as a Jew and consequently had to keep two Sabbaths, Saturday and Sunday, which meant confinement to his cell on both those days; no wonder if he got tired of his own thoughts and wanted to escape from them by coming to a place of worship where at least he would be in company and hear something. He was a notorious criminal and had been guilty of some profitable turf frauds. After he was liberated he got into fresh trouble, and it was announced in the papers that when confined in a Belgian prison he committed suicide by throwing himself from one of the upper landings on to the floor below. I had my own doubts about the truth of this, although (as they say) it was in the newspapers. He may have got it inserted for the purpose of hiding his identity. He was quite clever enough to manage this.

As well as the daily and Sunday services we had every two years a visit from the Bishop for a confirmation, when any prisoners who offered themselves, after a careful preparation on my part, extending over some six or eight weeks, were presented to the Bishop and duly confirmed in the presence of all the other prisoners. It was always an anxious time for me, especially when I had to decide as to the fitness or otherwise of the candidates, but I always found them most reasonable when I had to advise a man to postpone his confirmation, and although I had of course some disappointments in the after-conduct of my candidates, on the whole I was not sorry that I had allowed them to be confirmed and afterwards admitted to the Holy Communion. I was always the more satisfied when, as in some cases, they ended their lives in prison.

One case I recall in particular of a youth whom I baptized and prepared for Confirmation and admitted to the Holy Communion, who after two years of a consistent life was taken ill and died in the infirmary, receiving the Holy Communion at my hands the day before he died, and passing away in the faith and hope of a glorious resurrection.

146 A CHAPLAIN ON DARTMOOR It was always a test of their moral courage if they offered themselves for baptism, as I always administered it in the presence of the whole congregation after the second lesson of the afternoon service. On one occasion before a Confirmation I baptized five convicts and had no cause to regret it in either case.

That some unorthodox views were entertained is manifest from the following incident. At the time of a Confirmation I naturally spoke on the subject in my sermons, as well as on the importance of baptism. One day a man sent for me to tell me that he had listened to what I had said on these subjects, and wanted to be baptized.

" But," I said, " haven't you been baptized already in infancy? The probability is that you have, and if so, you can't be baptized again. Once enlisted into the army of Christ you are His soldier and servant unto your life's end."

" Oh yes," he said, "I know I have been baptized, but I want you to do it again, because I want to change my name. My name is Scamp, and I want to change it; what chance is there for a man called that? How would you like to be called Scamp?"

I told him the name was of no consequence if he didn't live up to it, and so the matter ended.

Our chapel itself was a large building with an uninterrupted view from end to end, and the distant moorland and hills could be seen through the large east window of unstained glass. It left much to be desired from a churchman's point of view. The walls were adorned by appropriate texts on tin scrolls, painted by a clever prisoner. And for further decoration we always had a beautiful collection of the choicest flowers on the altar. Several ladies, in answer to an advertisement I inserted in a church paper, agreed to supply me with a basket of flowers once a week. Up to the time of my leaving they very kindly fulfilled this promise, and our church was always decorated with most beautiful hot-house flowers, such as were rarely seen on Dartmoor.

As to the sermons they had to be short and to the point, if possible with one or two suitable illustrations. The selection of a subject was sometimes decided for me by the Gospel for the day or one of the lessons, and it was necessary to confine one's notes to a sheet of paper, as written sermons always seemed to fall rather flat. I 148 A CHAPLAIN ON DARTMOOR have sometimes had to trust to the inspiration of the moment, although it was rather a dangerous experiment. I remember once having taken notes with me for a prepared sermon, without having looked over the lessons beforehand, as I usually did. As it turned out the afternoon lesson was concerning Joseph in prison, and his interpretation of the dreams of the chief butler and the chief baker, the concluding verse of the chapter being " Yet did not the chief butler remember Joseph, but forgat him." This was too good a subject to miss, and the lesson ought to come home to many before me, so that my prepared notes were kept in my pocket, and whilst the men were singing the hymn before the sermon my mind was dwelling upon the subject of " Prison promises and how to keep them," illustrating their failure by the example of the chief butler in that far-off time in an Egyptian prison.

I once took for the subjects of my sermons all the prisoners mentioned in the Bible, and was surprised to find how many lessons of practical utility could be drawn from them. I could almost see the ears of my congregation prick up to listen, and there was marked attention when I gave out for my text I Kings xxii, 26-27, "And the king of Israel said, take Micaiah and carry him back unto Amon the governor of the city, and say, thus saith the king, put this fellow in the prison, and feed him with bread of affliction and with water of affliction until I come in peace." Later on I ranged, one by one, through the prisoners named in the Old and New Testaments, as Joseph, Paul and Silas, Peter, and many others. The notes for these sermons I wrote out fully afterwards, and sent them all up to the S. P. C. K. for publication. They were returned to me for some slight alterations, and by some mishap got mislaid and lost. I often wondered what became of them, as I never saw them again after I left the prison. I hope they were appreciated by anyone who found them, and had the patience to read them. They were hardly suitable for an ordinary congregation.

I do not know if other preachers do what I found it useful at times to do, viz., preach without a text. I suppose it would be considered somewhat unorthodox, but if one had a good subject for one's discourse it seemed to give one more freedom than when one was tied down to a text, 150 A CHAPLAIN ON DARTMOOR and at least freed one from the charge of wandering from it. In my case it came about in this way: I used sometimes to have a nightmare that I was in a pulpit with a large congregation in front of me, and to my horror found that I had lost my text and stood there speechless, while frantically searching for it, until to my relief I awoke. I thought I would test this by actual experience, and after doing so, and not finding the result so dreadful, I never had the nightmare again!

It is curious how a sort of electric sympathy exists between preacher and people, so that one can tell if people are interested or otherwise in what one is saying, and so also with other emotions. One morning at the ordinary service, when the prisoners were nearly all assembled, I noticed that something was happening out of the usual. Heads were turned and looks exchanged, which told me plainly that something unusual was happening. However I went through the service, and later in the day when visiting the men in their cells, I asked one of the more intelligent of the convicts what was the excitement in the chapel that morning.

noticed it. The men had the surprise of their lives."

" How so? " I asked; " I didn't see anything to surprise them."

" No sir, perhaps not," he said, " but you didn't recognise a new arrival as we did."

" Who was that? " I asked.

Why old N., the biggest fence (or receiver of stolen goods) in all London. Many of us have had dealings with him for years, and we always thought he was too rich and too clever to be caught. We were surprised, I can tell you, to see the police had got him at last, and to think he had come to join us whom he had cheated over and over again."

So long as everything went on smoothly, as it did during the years I officiated in the chapel, it was all very nice, but one never knew what might happen; it was like living in a powder magazine, that a spark might blow up at any time, and this was especially the case if one got a warning that something was going to happen. A well-conducted, decent prisoner once told me that there was going to be a row at the morning service, and he advised me at the first sign to go out at the vestry door, and take the Scripture 152 A CHAPLAIN ON DARTMOOR reader with me, as they did not wish to harm either of us.

" Will there be a fight? " I asked.

Yes," he replied, " and rather a bad one I am afraid."

" Then," I said, "I for one shall be there to see it out, although I'm much obliged for the information."

Nothing came of it, so I suppose they changed their minds, but such warnings tend to upset one's devotion.

As regards the subjects chosen for one's sermons I sometimes wished that a hint could be given from one's congregation. I believe that some clergymen adopt the plan of inviting any members of their congregation to put such requests in a box placed in the church so that the preacher may preach upon them, and enlighten the enquirer upon any matter that troubles him by explaining to the best of his ability from the Word of God. I did not venture to try this experiment on my versatile congregation, knowing beforehand the sort of requests I should receive, and the subjects that would be suggested, such as, for instance, "The influence of kindness on the part of man to man "; " The hardening effect of brutality upon the heart of man "; "Is imprisonment as now carried on in our prisons likely to do any good? "; " Bad food and its effect on mind and body "; " What are sermons and why are they preached? "; and many more of the same kind. So that I had to trust to my own judgment, and often found it a difficult task, after exhausting the lessons suggested by each Sunday's gospel, epistle, or lessons.

I don't suppose any man or woman out of prison has ever listened to so many sermons in ten years as a convict in one of our prisons. Two every Sunday, not counting any short addresses delivered on week days, amount in ten years to over a thousand, and there are many men who have had their Sundays in prison for longer periods than that. What a comfort it would be to the sower if he could only know that the more seed he scattered the larger would be the crop! The seed may be of the best, and the sower in earnest, but then there is the soil, and we have it on the highest authority that it was the honest and good heart that produced the good fruit, some thirty, some sixty, some a hundredfold. Well, all we had for our 154 A CHAPLAIN ON DARTMOOR encouragement was, "In the morning sow thy seed, and in the evening withhold not thy hand, for thou knowest not what shall prosper or whether they both shall be alike good, 5 and so leave the result to the Ruler of hearts.

Often when some kind friend has consented to take my place in the pulpit on Sunday I have been asked by him as to the subject of his sermon. What shall I preach about?"

" I must leave that to you," was my reply, "I can't tell you what to preach about, I can only tell you what not to preach about–the parable of the prodigal son–they have heard that so often that there is nothing you can say that they have not heard over and over again. And another thing I would add is, don't use long words, but only simple English words of one or two syllables. You may think this warning unnecessary, but I tell you it isn't, as I have heard many a sermon preached over the heads of a congregation owing to a forgetfulness of the fact that many in the congregation are unlearned and ignorant people."

A clergyman once had a clerical friend staying with him over Sunday, and gladly availed himself of the offer of his friend to preach for him in the morning. He told his friend that the congregation were mostly simple and unlearned folk, and so he said, "Don't use any long and hard words in your sermon where short and easy ones can be employed."

" All right said his friend, "Ill bear it in mind."

After service as they came out of church and were walking down the path to the vicarage, his friend turned to him with the remark, st I hope you were satisfied; did I carry out your instructions?: : No," said the vicar, "I don't think you did."

What do you mean? " said the preacher; " tell me any word that I used in my sermon that your people couldn't understand?"

" Amongst others," said his friend, " you used the word felicity. Not half my people would understand what felicity means; why couldn't you have said happiness, or better still, joy?

" Oh! that's nonsense," said the friend, " why it is a word used in the Prayer Book; anyone would know its meaning. Let us ask this farmer, he seems well-to-do, and fairly intelligent."

Accordingly they accosted the farmer, and 156 A CHAPLAIN ON DARTMOOR gradually approached the sermon, of which the farmer spoke in praise.

" You heard him use the word felicity," said the vicar, " and of course you know what it means?"

"Well," said the farmer, "I don't rightly know the exact meaning, but I know it's something inside a pig."

CHAPTER VI.

ESCAPES

NATURALLY the first thing that enters the mind of every convict arriving at the prison is, "What chance is there of escape? " and the grand open moor stretching away for miles in sight of all working outside in the garden or on the moor seems to beckon and point plainly to freedom. Some few now and again respond to the repeated invitation, only to be captured and disappointed, rewarded for the attempt by solitary confinement and a dose of bread and water. I have often been consulted by the men as to the chances of a successful attempt and have always told the same truth, that knowing what I do I should certainly never make the attempt, were I myself a prisoner, pointing to the fact that no one in the history of the modern prison has ever been successful in a final escape.

The only man who succeeded in evading capture for a long period was one who was at work in the chaplain's house, and evading the 158 A CHAPLAIN ON DARTMOOR notice of his warder slipped into the dressing-room, changed his convict dress for a full suit of clerical attire, walked out to the stable, and mounting the clerical cob, rode through the village, receiving and politely returning the salutes of any warder he met. He had the politeness, after a time, to return the pony and clothes with many thanks, to the owner. He got down to Teignmouth, and hoped to get a ship to take him out of the country, but through forgetful-ness he gave his landlady his stockings to wash, which gave him away, as she noticed the tell-tale red stripes, and recognised them as prison marked. He enjoyed his liberty for nearly six months, and when brought back told me his adventures, and blamed himself for having made such a foolish mistake.

Escapes when made always create a certain amount of excitement and disturbance in routine, both for the warders and prisoners, not forgetting the warders' wives, who know that in all probability their husbands will suffer for their negligence, as well as the prisoners for their folly.

Escapes have their comic as well as their tragic sides. Here is one of the former. I won't vouch for the truth of it, as it did not happen in my time, but at an earlier date, when discipline was not so strict as it became later on.

One afternoon when the recall bell rang, a party of men working on reclaiming the bogs, about a mile from " home," packed up their tools, and were marched back to the prison. On arrival, where a count is taken and each party is checked, it was found that one man was missing from the party just returned from the bogs. When it was found that old Smith was the runaway, every one was rather surprised, as he was a well-behaved convict and nearing the time for his discharge. Parties of warders armed were sent out in all directions, except to the particular bog where the man had been working all day, as it was naturally concluded he would not be there, but as far away as he could travel in the time. About 6-30, when the hunt was far advanced, some of the searchers being miles from home, to the surprise of the gate-keeper the old man arrived and asked to be admitted, as he said he wanted his tea.

Why, where have you been? J: asked the janitor, " we thought you had escaped."

" Escaped," he said, " where could I escape to?"

160 A CHAPLAIN ON DARTMOOR

Well, where have you been?!

" Nowhere; I was tired and after dinner it was very hot, so I lay down in the heather and went to sleep, and when I woke up there was no one about, so I got up and here I am, and I suppose youll let me in as I want my tea, and I hope cook has kept it hot for me!"

Another man I knew was sent to Dartmoor to do his punishment because he made his escape from Parkhurst, in the Isle of Wight, and was at liberty for more than a week, when he was recaptured by trying to take the train from one of the principal stations. He had kept himself alive by milking cows in the early morning and hiding during the day. The kindness of a farmer and his wife led to his undoing. He found a nice heap of straw deposited against a rick, and crawling under it slept till morning. He had made a sort of peep-hole, so that he could see what was going on in the farmyard, and soon the farmer's wife came out and fed her fowls, and then to his dismay came towards his hiding place, knelt down, and put her arm under the straw in search of an egg which her favourite hen left there in a well-used nest. When instead of the expected egg, she felt the boot of my friend she gave a loud scream, and rushed for the house. My friend tumbled out of his straw lair, and bolted down the field on one side of the hedge, followed by the farmer on horseback on the other. He was soon overtaken, and instead of being roughly treated, he was hailed by the farmer crying out to him, "Don't be afraid; I see who you are–the escaped convict that they are hunting the island for. Well my man, I expect you are hungry; now come back to the house and have breakfast with me."

Well, I wasn't likely to do that"–so ran my friend's tale–" so I said, If it is all the same to you I should prefer to have it here if youll bring it.

Of course I will, but you need not think I would give you up.

Well in a short time I saw him coming back carrying a basket, and afterwards found it contained eggs and bacon, and a bottle of hot coffee! I thanked him for his kindness, and was leaving him, when he called me back, and said, Now if you want a bed to-night, don't disturb the old hen, but come to my house and Ill put you up.

When I declined his kind offer, he added, 162 A CHAPLAIN ON DARTMOOR

Well remember my offer if it turns out to be a wet night, and I think it will be.

" And it was; so that about 10 o'clock I could stand it no longer and thought I would risk it and walked back and claimed his hospitality. He gave me supper and a bed, and treated me most kindly. It was suggested that I might likc to write to my wife, and without any thought of the risk I ran, I foolishly wrote her a letter, on paper stamped with the farmer's address, which, of course, led to the betrayal of myself and my good friend. I never knew what happened to him, but I fear he would suffer for his Christian treatment of a fellow creature in dire distress. I left next day, and hid in a bathing machine, and on two occasions heard the warders as they passed discussing the probability of my capture."

He got tired of the life and determined to get away by train and boat. Having obtained clothes and discarded his broad arrow uniform, he marched on to the platform of one of the stations. He found there the deputy governor and other officials, and had to pass through them. He said if he could have kept his nerve he believed they would have failed to recognise him,

but lie could not carry it through, and in his panic made a bolt into the tunnel at the end of the platform, and was captured on emerging at the other end.

I remember another young fellow, smart, good tempered, and well behaved, who was sent to us for a sharp spell of bread and water for breaking out of prison at the Isle of Wight. He and a companion managed to get out one night, and found an entrance to the doctor's house, where there had been a big supper party, and the table left with all the remnants of the supper laid promiscuously, as the guests had left them. In telling me the man said, "Why, sir, it was just as if the doctor had expected us, and meant to give us the best welcome that he could, knowing that a good feed was just the one thing we convicts would appreciate. The table was laid, and there were the plentiful remains of turkey, chicken and ham, and sausage, in addition to tarts, custards, cakes, and trifle, with large silver flagons of wine. Although the last was weak and watery, it was good enough to wash down the eatables, all sufficient to make one's mouth water for many a day since. We sat down and ate and ate and ate, as only two hungry convicts 164 A CHAPLAIN ON DARTMOOR could, after the meagre prison fare which we had had for a year or more. At last, fairly fed up, I could eat no more, even with such dainties spread out before me. I couldn't look at another bite.

" Try a bit more of this cold turkey, Bill, said my companion from his seat at the other side of the table.

" No thank you, my friend, I couldn't eat a bit more to save my life."

And so after pocketing what they could, they left the house; but were seen by the coastguard, chased and captured.

It was my duty to visit the man every morning in the penal cells whilst he was undergoing his punishment for the attempt, and of course I said what I could to cheer him up. He took it all in good part for some days, but one morning I found him in an unusually depressed state.

" Hullo," I said, " what's the matter with you this morning? You mustn't give way, but bear up like a man. It will soon be over now."

" So I will; it isn't that, chaplain." Well, what is it then? Can I do anything to help you?"

" No; what I can't bear is the thought of that supper table and that I didn't have a bit more when I had the chance. The thought of that cold turkey and the other things haunts me, and that I could have been such a fool as to say No! when invited to have just a little bit more. I keep thinking and thinking about it and oh! how I wish I had had another slice of that ham."

Another old man made a bolt for it in a thick fog, when his party was returning to the prison from work outside. I was out walking with my wife, and about a mile from home heard one or two rifle shots, which I knew could mean but one thing–an escape!

" Look out I said, " we may see a runaway; he will very likely cross the road we are on." The fog, however, was too thick and although I heard afterwards from the man himself that he passed only a few yards ahead of us we saw nothing of him in the fog, and he made his way across the moor and down the valley to Dartmeet, and over the hill towards Heytor and Ilsington, which it turned out afterwards was his home. When he arrived home, his wife would not admit him, but drove him off with threats; so he had to hide and skulk about for some days, as the search parties were hot on his track. For want 166 A CHAPLAIN ON DARTMOOR of food he broke into a farmhouse and helped himself to what he could find in the larder and was eventually caught and brought back to the prison.

I had a long talk with him next morning, and though I found him rather sulky and morose, I at last heard from him some of his adventures. When captured he had shed his prison clothes, and had dressed himself in old rags that he had found on various scarecrows in the fields, and he had also a common garden hoe. This was found by him to be a very useful tool for disguise, as when travelling across fields by day, if anyone came in sight he set to work hoeing up weeds. When he was brought to trial an old farmer came to see him. and recognised him as a man he had seen, as he rode past, hoeing up weeds in a stubble field. Why drat," he said, " that's the man I saw hoeing Farmer C."s stubble. It struck me as something new, and I meant to ask my friend Farmer C. what was up, when he employed a labourer to hoe his stubble."

It was quite a fortnight before he was caught; he gave the warders a lot of trouble, and kept them out on the prowl night and day, far from home, so that I think they were a little bit vexed when the old chap got off very lightly–through being brought to trial before a lenient and reasonable judge–on the double charge of breaking out of prison and of burglary.

" Well take him on the first charge." Yes, my Lord, he ran away in a fog, and escaped from the warders in charge of him."

" Well," said the judge, " that is only what anyone would do that had the chance. It is the duty of the prison authorities to keep him in prison, and not to give him the chance; I can't see that the prisoner has committed much of a crime in that. How about the second charge– the burglary. What did he do? Broke into a house and stole some food? Did he do any damage or hurt anybody? 5:

" No, my Lord, only stole some cold chicken and bread."

"Well," said the judge, "it seems to me that this follows naturally on the first offence; if a man escapes from prison he must steal some food or die of hunger. If he had done any serious damage, or injured anyone, that would be a different matter; but as it is,

I can't view either the escape or the burglary as deserving of a heavy sentence. How long has the prisoner to do of his present sentence?"

168 A CHAPLAIN ON DARTMOOE

" Two years, my Lord."

Then, as the law obliges me to sentence you for burglary, I sentence you to two years' imprisonment for the same, to run concurrently with your present unexpired sentence!"

An amusing incident happened during a recent escape of two convicts. They had been at liberty for some days, and the news had spread far and wide, arousing no little uneasiness amongst the small householders on the moor. The fear of. visit induced one good lady of my acquaintance to deposit, before going to bed, some food and clothes in the passage, in readiness for any interlopers, who might be pleased with such forethought and so take their departure without waking the inmates.

In the midst of this alarm caused by its being known that two desperate convicts were at large, one dark night two of the warders in plain clothes were on the watch at a bridge, which it was thought the convicts might cross. At last a footstep was heard approaching, and soon the pedestrian was in the hands of the warders, who were proceeding to fasten his wrists. The man whom they thus mistook for the convict was an inoffensive small farmer returning home from market, perhaps a little market merry, and lie on his part mistook the two warders for the escaped convicts, so when they seized him he was desperately frightened, knowing from hearsay that men in their plight would stick at nothing to obtain food and clothes.

" Look here, my good fellows, I know who you be, you'm them two chaps who have run away from Princetown. Now don't e go to hurt me. I'm only a poor man, but Ill give you my clothes and all Ive got if you won't murder me. You won't be so cruel when I tell you Ive a wife and childer waiting up for me at home, and they won't care if I come home naked, so as I come home alive."

A notable escape was made by a man named Goodwin, who disappeared in a fog, and was not recaptured for some days. The man was very intelligent, and a bit of a poet. I had some talks with him on his return to the prison, and at my request he wrote a very interesting account of his flight and adventures in a poem of about thirty verses. He could only write it on his slate, and I copied it out on paper. I wish I had it by me to transcribe here, but when he left, at the end of his sentence, he wrote persistently asking me to 170 A CHAPLAIN ON DARTMOOR send him the copy. I was too busy at the time to write out another copy, and so sent him the only one I had made, as he said that the editor of one of the dailies had offered him a good sum of money for it. I never saw it in print, so doubt if it came up to the editor's expectation. I thought it very good.

The man made his way from the prison straight for Two Bridges and Post Bridge. There he broke into a house and procured food and a change of clothes. He told me that it was an awful night, wet and windy and pitch dark. Resting under walls and walking, when dawn came he found himself once more just in front of the prison, having unwittingly retraced his footsteps. He said he was so done up that he was much inclined to give it up, but as he had so far evaded the warders he thought he might have a chance if he could get down to Plymouth. That night he found himself in the outskirts of Tavistock, where he broke into a house and feasted on the remains of a turkey left over from the Christmas dinner. He then took the railway track for his guide and ultimately reached Devonport, where he was recognised and handed over to the police, who delivered him to the warders who had followed him down the line. He was placed in a wagonette and driven smartly through the crowded street, greeted with the cheers of the onlookers, a very improper but very natural recognition of his pluck and cleverness He arrived " home " just as I was leaving the prison after the Sunday afternoon service, and just outside the prison I found most of the inhabitants of Princetown, who gave him a cheer of welcome as he passed under the gloomy portal with its inscription " Par cere subjectis " overhead. He was thoroughly done up, and when I went in to see him an hour afterwards, I found him tucked up in bed in the hospital fast asleep, from which he never woke until about 11 o'clock next morning. " Nevermore as long as I live will I try and escape; it was awful."

He behaved himself very well until he was liberated at the end of his sentence. He wrote me several nice letters from Cape Town, where he seems to have got work as an engineer until his death, which took place some three years afterwards. At Easter, after hearing the Story of the Cross sung in chapel, he wrote me the following imitation of it. When Sir Henry Acland was visiting the prison, in which he was 172 A CHAPLAIN ON DARTMOOR much interested, I showed him the verses. After carefully reading them, he handed them back to me with only one word, " wonderful! J3

STOEY OF THE CROSS

See from the Judgment Hall
Jesus led forth, Now to be crucified
On the cross.
See at each weary step,
As He draws near, They smite Him with hands
Without fear.
Oh! hear the mocking scoffs
At Jesus hurled; At Christ the Lord and King
Of the world.
His diadem of thorns Is on His brow; Before Him in mocking
Jest they bow.
There at the gate they meet
Simon, who shares With Jesus the weary load
Which He bears.
Now to Calvary mount,
Ah! must it be That Jesus there must die
All for me?
Yes, there between two thieves
My Saviour hangs, For my sins He bears those
Bitter pangs.
See, the cruel nails
Are driven in Those sacred hands and feet
For my sin.

Now is the sharp spear
Thrust in Thy side, Water and blood flows out; Oh!
Sacred tide.
Yes in that flowing tide
Of precious blood, My sins are washed away
Through Thy love.
I see Thy anguish sore,
Thy bitter pain; Oh! Saviour mine, for sinners
Thou art slain.
174 A CHAPLAIN ON DARTMOOR In Thy sore agony
Upon the tree, Thy haughty foes with scorn
Rail at Thee.
Now hear those gracious words,
So good and true, "Forgive them for they know not What they do."
Oh! hear the dying thief In earnest prayer, Pleading with the Lord Who
Hangeth there.
What words of comfort those
To sinners' plea, "With Me in paradise Thou shalt be."
Standing afar off, but
Gazing on Thee, Thy few kinsfolk mourn Thy
Grief to see.
" I thirst," ah! cruel pang.
And at Thy call They bring vinegar and Bitter gall.
It is finished; Lord, for
Me Thou hast died; Now in heaven Thou art
Glorified.
Thy foes with trembling fear
Behold Thy powers; Darkness falls on the land
For three hours.
Yes, Thy power is seen,
For in the gloom The saints that sleep arise
From the tomb.
The vail is rent, the rocks
Burst asunder; Thy foes in silent awe
Behold in wonder.
Oh! Lord, blest Eedeemer,
Thou art my stay, Guide and keep me in the
Narrow way.
As at Thy cross I kneel.
Oh! hear my prayer, In heaven may I be to
Meet Thee there.
176 A CHAPLAIN ON DARTMOOR

That men should make the attempt to break out of prison surprises no one, but when a man has finished his sentence and is enjoying his freedom, it is a little surprising that he should come back, and break into the prison. But this really took place one night.

We had a mulatto for some years in the prison. A very troublesome, violent-tempered man when he was put out of humour by what he considered ill treatment on the part of a warder. One night as the governor entered the prison gate for his nightly round of inspection, which must always take place after 11 p. m., the alarm bell at the gate rang violently. This bell is connected with a wire running round the inside of the outer wall of the prison.

" Hullo! " said the governor, " what's up? What does that mean?"

" Oh," said the gate-keeper, " it's most likely a cat jumping down into the prison after rats, and he's hit the wire in his descent."

" Call out the guard," says the governor, " and search the workshops and other buildings."

And it was fortunate that they did so, for at the top of a ladder leading up to the carpenter's shop they discovered the mulatto trying his best to kindle a fire with some loose shavings. When questioned he said he had come to burn down the prison and murder the chief warder! He was handcuffed and given over to the village constable to be tried by the civil court at Tavistock. I went down to see him next morning and found the constable considerably troubled by his responsibility and the violence of his prisoner. He demurred to my request to see him, and said the man was threatening murder to anyone who came near him!

" Well," I said, " unlock the cell; he won't murder me."

With a little persuasion the door was opened, and I was admitted to the prisoner. He was certainly looking rather obstreperous, but when he recognised me he subsided, and said he was glad to see me. I asked him what he meant by acting as he had done, and getting himself into such a serious scrape. He told me he had come to murder the chief warder and would do it yet.

" Now," I said, " don't be a fool; if you talk like that youll get another severe sentence. Take my advice and say nothing, and you may get off lightly, as I don't know what they can give you for getting into a prison; most people are only too anxious to keep out."

178 A CHAPLAIN ON DARTMOOR

After telling the policeman's wife to bring him a good breakfast of eggs and bacon, which he ate hungrily whilst I talked, I left him. I read of his trial at Exeter shortly afterwards, and as he didn't take my advice and hold his tongue, but breathed out threatenings and slaughter against the chief warder, he got a stiff sentence, and died in captivity, notorious as the man who broke into a prison.

Because it was considered impossible for a man to escape from Millbank, in the very heart of London, the officers may perhaps have become slack, but I knew a man who successfully accomplished the trick, and no one knows to this day how it was done, save the man himself and those who helped him.

One morning I visited a man in whom I was much interested, for according to his own statement between his sentences in Dartmoor he had gone through the Candahar campaign with General Roberts. I found him considerably put out, owing to a visit he had just received from two detectives who had come to find out how he got out of Millbank, and particularly who had helped him, as without help from within it was concluded he could not possibly have done it.

He refused to give them any information in spite of many promises and threats.

" Well, if you won't tell us who did help you, will you tell us who didn't?"

" I won't tell you anything," was his last word, and they left him.

" Don't you think I was right, sir," he asked. I won't say what my answer was, but he seemed pleased with it. He gave me a good many details as to the manner of his escape, but none as to his helpers.

" But," I said, " when you got outside what could you do in your prison dress, and all the people in the streets?"

Well," he said, " of course it was night, and rather dark, and I made it darker by covering myself all over with soot, so that as a chimney sweep I had no difficulty in keeping out of people's way; they kept out of mine!"

One summer afternoon I went with my wife to pay a call on some visitors lodging in the village, and as I sat in the window a warder on horseback dashed full gallop down the street, past the window. I knew at once what that meant, and with some feeble excuse got up to go outside. What's the matter? " they exclaimed.

180 A CHAPLAIN ON DARTMOOR

" Nothing much, I expect, but I'm going out to see."

As soon as we were outside, we found the village in a turmoil. All the children were just released from school; lots of visitors who had come up for the day and all the inhabitants formed a crowd that nearly filled the street. We then learned that when a large number of prisoners who had been busy haymaking had finished for the afternoon, and the recall bell had sounded, after laying their tools in the usual chests, seven of them, instead of falling in, had jumped the stone wall and made a bolt for liberty. It was a reckless and foolish thing to do, for they were surrounded by the civil guard, who were posted at intervals some distance away, and although there was some shooting no one was hurt, and some of the runaways got past the guards and were soon captured. Whilst we were discussing their chances, we heard a cry, "Theyve got them; here they come! " to my great surprise, for I never thought that the warders would bring their captives through the village. That, however, being the nearest way to the prison, they took it and round the corner at the bottom of the street came warders and convicts, apparently without any order, but all in a crowd. They were soon surrounded and followed by the mass of spectators, school children, visitors, and villagers all marching confusedly together. There was laughing and joking, and apparently none seemed to be enjoying the joke so much as the prisoners, who appeared to be having the time of their lives, and were evidently the heroes in the play. We followed for some distance up the road, until we came to a small cluster of women who had come up from the adjacent barracks to see what all the noise was about. These were the only people with long faces, who did not seem to enjoy the scene quite as much as the others.

! Why aren't you glad at their speedy capture?" we enquired.

" There's another side to it that we are thinking about. Someone is bound to get into trouble over this as well as the convicts. Theyll be punished for escaping, and the warders will be punished for letting them escape, and who knows but those warders may be our husbands. There's no fun for us in an escape."

Here is another account of an escape in which without knowing it at the time I gave a helping hand to the runaway.

182 A CHAPLAIN ON DARTMOOR

Located in the end cell on No. 2 landing in V prison was a very troublesome and unruly prisoner named H. The cell on his landing had no view beyond the high prison wall, so that there was no possibility of communicating with anyone outside the prison, whereas from the top landing a signal could be made to anyone on the Rundlestone Road, about half a mile distant from the prison. By some means he had arranged with friends outside to meet him with a motor car and clothes, when a signal was given from the top story of No. V prison. The waving of a white cloth from any one of these windows would mean that H. would break out that night, and hoped to meet his friends at a certain hour at the appointed time and place.

Now as he could not make the signal himself, owing to the position of his cell, it was necessary that he should get it made by a fellow prisoner located on the top landing, and he would let him know when he had made up his mind for the attempt. But how was he to do this? Once the signal was made, he must go that night or not at all. And here it was that I was unwittingly called in to complete the arrangement for the signalling.

One Saturday morning I was mounting the iron stairs in No. V, when H., who was doing some odd jobs on the landing, came over to me and blandly asked me if I was going on to the top landing; if so, would I take a French dictionary which he had done with up to W., in cell 275, who was very anxious to possess one? At first I refused, telling him that it was irregular, and that he had only to put out the book, and the schoolmaster would give it to the next man in turn. He pleaded very hard, saying how much the man wanted it, so that at last I yielded and said, "Well, give me the book, and your book card, so that I can mark it off yours, and enter it on W."s."

When I reached W."s cell and told him what I had brought him at H."s request, at first he seemed surprised, but then, recovering himself, thanked me profusely, saying how much he wanted the dictionary, and how H. had promised if possible to let him have it. I had some misgivings about the matter, and had looked carefully through the book to see that there was no writing, or marks on any of the leaves.

This was on Saturday morning, but on Sunday morning H."s cell was found to be empty, and 184 A CHAPLAIN ON DARTMOOR the prisoner gone. I began to consider if there was anything in this book transfer connected with the escape, and I found out afterwards, from the man himself, that there was. He confessed to me that he had agreed with W., when they were both at work in the quarry, that when W. received the dictionary he was to show the signal to the watchers outside as an intimation that the escape would be made that night. In accordance with this, H. that night broke the whole of the ventilator with its frame out of the window of his cell, tied the sheets of his bed together, and lowered himself into the prison yard. With the help of a plank he scaled the outside wall, and made off to the appointed rendezvous. Here he waited for some hours for his friends, but for some unknown cause they failed him, and he was obliged to make off on his own account. So hiding by day and travelling by night, he reached Chagford, where he was captured by a farmer, and brought back to prison by the warders who had gone out to hunt him as soon as his escape was discovered on the Sunday morning.

Soon after his return I interviewed him, as was my custom. He met me with a smile as I entered his cell, and the first thing I asked him was: " However did you get out of your cell through that small opening?"

" Well," he said, " at the first try I stuck fast, but wriggling myself back into my cell, I stripped, threw my clothes out into the yard, and stark naked I found I could just squeeze through; but it was a tight fit I can tell you. Of course, when my friends failed me I knew it was all up, but I had an awful night on the moor. Wind and rain, and in crossing a river I was nearly drowned."

Well, I am glad for your own sake that we have got you safely back, as I was afraid of the consequences, if you put up a fight, as I thought you would before being captured. You gave in quite sensibly when that farmer challenged you."

" So would you," he replied, " if a dog had you by the leg, and a man with a loaded gun was pointing at you, and swearing he would shoot if you showed fight. But there was no fight left in me; that night on the moor knocked me out, and I wasn't sorry to be caught. I was done."

Well, now," I said, " one more question, Where does the French dictionary come in in this tale?"

186 A CHAPLAIN ON DARTMOOK

He laughed and said, "Better not ask me. I daresay W. will tell you "–as he did later on, and it was as I have written in this account of another escape from Dartmoor.

FOGS.

From the instances of escapes, or rather attempts at escape, it must not be gathered that all such attempts are the results of much planning and scheming, for many are just the result of opportunity and a sudden impulse. I knew one man who was captured after two or three days wandering about the moor, never more than two or three miles from the prison. He told me that he had never seriously considered the idea, and always regarded it as an impossibility, seeing the situation of the prison in the middle of a wide moor, and the difficulty in regard to obtaining food and a change of clothes, and yet he was tempted to try it on the spur of the moment and an unlooked-for opportunity. Fogs are very prevalent, and often come down unexpectedly, and without much warning. In such a case all men working outside the prison are at once formed up in their parties and marched into the prison, or to any adjacent building, until, perhaps, the fog lifts, and they can go on with their work.

The party in which my friend was working was gathered into a large wooden shed open in front, but boarded up behind. The men were formed up in two rows inside the shed, and the warders stood outside in front, facing the two rows of men drawn up inside. My friend told me they had stood thus waiting for the fog to lift, when looking round he saw there was a door just behind him, and outside that door there was a stone wall and a fir plantation. With his hand behind him he tried the latch, and found the door would open if the latch were lifted. A sudden impulse to escape seized him, and when the warder's attention was taken off, or the fog prevented him from seeing the men in the rear rank, my friend opened the door, slipped out, and jumping the stone wall, got unperceived in the dense fog into the spinney, and made his way out to the moor.

At first he was not missed, but when it was decided to march the party into the prison his absence was noticed, and the hue and cry was raised. He wandered about, hiding in the tors, and was not captured until two or three days later, having been first seen by the engine driver of the train on the Princetown railway. He told me he was not sorry to be brought back 188 A CHAPLAIN ON DARTMOOR
" home," as he had had a bad time, sleeping out, and hungry all the time.

Another case of opportunity prompting the sudden thought of escape is that of a man of whom it was said at the time that he was the last man in the prison that the warders would have suspected of any such intention. He had only a few months of a three years' sentence to serve. He was of a cheerful disposition, and responded with alacrity to any order given by the officers. Obedient, attentive, and seeming determined to make the best of a bad business, he gave no trouble of any kind, and so a certain amount of trust was placed in him. On no single occasion had he ever been reported for any breach of prison rules. That he would ever be foolish enough to break the most important rule of all, "Thou shalt not run away," was not for a moment thought likely by the warders under whose care he was working.

This work on the 31st October consisted in repairing the road and curbstone just outside the chaplain's quarters, in front of a large block of buildings occupied by the warders and their families. The weather was dull and misty, with occasional showers of rain. Work, however, was continued, as it would be an easy job to march the party back to the prison, if the weather got worse, the prison gates being only about 300 yards from the place where they were working. The entrance gates leading into the chaplain's yard and garden were thrown open for the admission of the carriage of some visitors, and only a field lay between the entrance and the moor. It was the open gate that put it into the head of the man to make the attempt. One short run and he was free. Taking up a spade he quietly detached himself from the party, apparently with the intention of getting some mortar, but when opposite the open gates he dropped the implement and made a dash across the yard, garden and field, and scrambling over a high turf fence reached the open moor. He rambled about amongst the tors for the rest of that day and the following night, but being unable to obtain food he became too hungry to hold out, and so came back and gave himself up to the first warder he met and was duly punished, for the first time in his prison life.

The fogs which come on so suddenly are most puzzling and difficult to surmount for any who happen to be caught on the open moor without a 190 A CHAPLAIN ON DARTMOOR guide or compass. I remember once in September meeting two women about 11 o'clock, when out shooting. There had been a dense fog over the moor the night before, and it had only just partially cleared when I encountered these two dishevelled objects, looking draggled, wet, and most forlorn. On coming nearer I discovered one to be the school mistress of the Huccaby school, and a friend. When I asked them what was the matter, they told me they had been out on the moor all night. They had started from Huccaby the night before to walk across, by a footpath, to Princetown to attend the harvest festival at church. When they were half way there a dense fog came on, and they got off the footpath and were quite lost in the darkness and fog. They could find no rocks to shelter them, and were rambling about all night, and had only just got out on to the road as the fog lifted. They looked half dead, and I advised them to get home as quickly as possible, and get into a warm bed and stop there. On enquiring a day or two later I found they were none the worse for their adventure.

I was once myself completely lost and turned round by a sudden fog when I was one day after snipe in one of the wildest parts of the moor, between Post Bridge and Cranmere Pool. I had a young friend with me, and as birds were fairly plentiful we had not noticed the gradual oncoming of the mist until we were completely enveloped, and could only see a yard or two ahead.

" We had better turn back," I said, " and make our way down the gully we came up, which will lead us to the Leat, and that will guide us home. But although we searched, and searched, we could not find any sign of the gully, and realised that we were lost, and might, perhaps, be out all night, for it was getting late in the afternoon, and if darkness came on with the fog we should be in an awkward fix. After tramping about for some time we stumbled on to a small trickle of water.

" Now," I said, " we shall be all right. If we follow this it must lead down to the river."

We plodded on for miles, following the little stream in all its windings, and at last came below the fog and discerned in the distance some rough buildings.

" Why," said my companion, " that must be the powder mills."

192 A CHAPLAIN ON DARTMOOR

" Nonsense," I said, " the powder mills are behind us. We have been travelling the other direction."

But it turned out to be the mills, and all the time we had been walking due west, and I thought we were walking due east. We were completely turned round. After this I took care to carry a compass with me, and have more than once by its help steered straight for home without any misgivings about being lost.

The following was written by the wife of a friend who was caught in a fog on the moor on a search for Cranmere Pool:–

One day two parsons started forth
To walk to Cranmere Pool, The weather was not really hot,
Nor was it very cool.
They walked and talked for hours and hours
As only parsons can, Until it seemed as though they'd trudged
From Beersheba to Dan.
At last they reached the pool and Lo!
With disappointment keen, One friend exclaims, "And is this all
At Cranmere to be seen?
" A horrid dirty muddy hole,
Surrounded by a bog, Ill never bring a friend again, I wouldn't bring a dog.
" I thought at least there'd be a shop,
Where we could get a snap Of something good to eat or drink, Or maybe take a nap."

"I'm sorry," said the other friend, "But we have seen the sight Of Cranmere Pool, and that's enough To satisfy me quite.

" We now must turn our footsteps home,

The mist is coming fast, But we shall surely reach the road Before the day is past."

But now, alas! the fog had come,

They could not see their way (In fogs on Dartmoor one would think

Twas night instead of day).

One parson ever led the way,

He went at breakneck speed, But knowing best this moorland wild,

Twas natural he should lead.

" Oh! do not go so fast," he heard, In accents from behind, "You certainly will break your leg,

Or neck, if you don't mind."

Twas useless; still he rushed along,

As thinking of his wife, And knowing she would anxious be

He went as for his life.

194 A CHAPLAIN ON DARTMOOR

His friend behind– a bachelor he–

To cheer their spirits sad, Sang " Wait until the clouds roll by"

In tones both loud and glad.

But when the clouds did not roll by, And when all hope grew dim,

He gallantly led up the rear By shouting out a hymn.

" Now you will have to jump," he heard

His friend ahead sing out, "Be careful, steady, come along,

Mind out what youre about."

We sometimes find it difficult To practise what we preach,

And so the good advice was lost; The ground he could not reach.

But down he went seven feet or more,

And into water fell, His friend behind he heard the splash

And simply gave a yell.

" Oh! tell me are you still alive?

My friend, oh! tell me do, Whatever will become of me, What has become of you?"

He scrambled out all wet and cold

And started off once more To lead the way o'er Dartmoor wilds

As he had done before.

At length, as over cows they fell,

And into holes they stepped, As bruised, and cold, and hungry they

Oer crags and torrents leapt,

They felt they must do something more

To try and find the way, So shouted loud, "Help, help, were lost "–

Twas all those two could say.

But 'twas enough, a dog began

To bark, and howl, and whine, And as they turned to where he was

A light was seen to shine.

They found a hut, they found a friend,
Who very kindly showed Them (by the help of s. d.)
How they could gain the road.
Then weary, faint, yet thankful, they
Procured a market cart, And once again did s. d.
Enable them to start.
They reached Princetown at 2 a. m.,
And found when they got there, Their friends all waiting anxiously,
And nearly in despair.
Around the kitchen fire we sat,
And dried and fed those two, We said, "Next time you go such tramps
Well send a guide with you."
196 A CHAPLAIN ON DARTMOOR
And you who read this doleful tale
On days wet, hot, or cool, If you must wander on the moor,
Don't go to Cranmere Pool.

The fogs are most deceptive and very tricky. They come on unexpectedly, and change the whole aspect of the surroundings. They magnify all things; hills comparatively small appear as high mountains, and a small bird like a snipe looks as big as a pigeon. One of the prettiest sights to be seen in the summer is when, with a bright sun overhead and a cloudless blue sky, the whole surface of the moor is seen to be steaming; spirals of mist, with intervals, rising like steam from the ground. Of equal beauty is another scene which is caused by dense fog in the winter with a hard frost congealing the drops of moisture on the end of every blade of grass, heather or shrub, so that a fairy diamond hangs on every particle of grass or bough. This is called the " Himmell," and is only to be seen occasionally. I have only seen it twice, but would go far to see it again.

The " Brocken " I have only seen once. One afternoon I walked up to the top of Hessary, the highest tor in the neighbourhood. Over the moor behind me was to be seen the smoke of Plymouth, and the estuary of the Tamar, with the sea beyond, all in bright sunshine; in front of me, looking east, was a wide valley bounded by a hill known as Bairdown, but invisible by reason of a dense fog, which filled the far side of the valley and rose like a dark wall higher than the opposite hill. As I reached the top of Hessary and looked across to this bank of mist there appeared the figure of a giant silhouetted on the wall of mist, as a picture on a screen. On first seeing it I was amazed, and did not first realise what it was. I had read of the Brocken which travellers had seen in the Alps, but I had never seen or heard of such a sight on Dartmoor. However, I was not left long in doubt, because as soon as I moved the figure moved, when I took off my hat and bowed the enormous figure returned my salute, and when I raised my arm and stick the figure did the same. For some half an hour I went through various antics, and watched with interest the corresponding movements of the Brocken. The performance came to an end by the setting of the sun behind me, and as at a theatre at the dropping of the curtain the scene vanished; there was only the curtain of fog in the valley, but no sunlight to throw the figure on the screen.

CHAPTEK VII.

PUNISHMENTS

A FAMOUS novelist once called upon me to obtain some local colour and information to help him in a novel he was about to write, which contained an account of a man who was sentenced to a term of penal servitude, and at the end of his term of imprisonment returned home to his wife. Would she recognize him? How many years would so change him in appearance that the wife would not know him? He thought twelve years, but I advised fifteen at the least. It is difficult to say; so much depends upon the physique and complexion, growth of hair, etc. Anything more disfiguring and disguising than the dress and tonsure of the man in prison it is impossible to imagine, and some of them feel it acutely, especially when a friend or relative is allowed to visit them, and they see how shocked their visitor is when faced with the grotesque Guy Fawkes opposite and realises that that is the man he has known outside in decent garments.

The vicar of a town church called on me one day with a permit to see a certain prisoner who had once been his organist. I went with him, and left him at the room where these interviews take place.

After about half an hour he joined me in my office. " Well! " he exclaimed, "I could not have believed it if I had not seen it with my own eyes, how you can completely change a man, not only in appearance but in manner. I know that is the man I came to see, because he spoke of people and events that no one else could have known, but when I was told that that creature in fustian and cropped head was the man that I knew, and who was my organist for many years– well, I could not believe it. Why, when I knew him he was always nicely and neatly dressed, frock coat, flower in button-hole, top hat, well-polished boots, etc., and the man was good looking and well groomed, with light moustache and beard. It is simply staggering to one's mind to recall his picture, and to put that man in front of me and tell me that's M. Well, well!"

Certainly the dress is very ugly, and although for the sake of preventing escapes some distinctive dress must be worn, surely something less 200 A CHAPLAIN ON DARTMOOE outrageous than the knickers and short jacket, covered with broad arrows, could be devised. It must destroy all self-respect to be thus hideously clothed, and I believe some slight alterations would not be difficult, and would make all the difference, both to the appearance and the feelings of the men. I have often wondered who was responsible for the present design. Was it copied from a scare-crow, or Guy Fawkes?

I was always most thankful that although we had many murderers with long sentences, we had no hangings in our prison. From what I gathered from a chaplain of another prison, nothing so upset the nerves of all the officials as the case of men under sentence of death, the most unconcerned apparently being the condemned man himself. The chaplain himself, who had attended more executions than any other man in the kingdom except the executioner, told me that it. was always the most upsetting experience of his life, and one that was never got over by its frequency. He said that the only cure for its awful nerve-racking was a change of scene, and that whenever possible, he always made a point of getting away after the horror of the execution to some fresh scene abroad; going straight away from the prison to the railway, and taking passage to Calais or to some foreign port; but even with this change it took him a week or ten days to rally and become his normal self. I was glad to escape this ordeal during my long term of prison experience, and we were also spared the pain of witnessing the painful scenes of a flogging. Once I very nearly, through forgetfulness, was present when a flogging took place. I came on the scene just as the officials had finished strapping the man to the triangle. It was in the prison where the men were confined under punishment, and it was part of my duty to visit all these men every morning. I blundered in quite forgetting there was a flogging to take place that morning. As I entered and took a few steps forward I came face to face with an unfortunate man tied to the triangle, waiting for the first stroke of the cat. As long as I live I shall never forget that man's face or its expression. I had often heard the saying " In a blue funk," but had never before seen an example of it. I saw it then, and hope I may never see it again. As soon as I realised what was taking place I made an undignified bolt for 202 A CHAPLAIN ON DARTMOOR the door, and escaped before the first stroke fell on the wretch's bare back.

Flogging with the cat is a cruel punishment, and has almost ceased in our prisons, as it has quite in the army and navy; and a much milder form of flogging has taken its place, viz., flogging with the birch, which is not much worse than what we were familiar with at school fifty years ago, and even this can only be inflicted by the sanction of the visiting justices for such serious offences as an assault upon a warder. In such cases I think the anticipation over-night is the worst part of the punishment, and most trying to the nerves of the culprit.

If I am asked whether I think any good comes of flogging, I should say in answer much harm would come of it if flogging were quite abolished, and I should quote the saying of the American judge who in answer to the culprit before him, whom he had just sentenced for stealing a horse, protesting that it was hard for a man to be hanged for such a crime, told him, "I don't sentence you to be hanged for stealing a horse, but rather to prevent other men from stealing horses." And whatever may be said as to the brutalising effect upon the culprits who have already displayed their brutality by some cruel assault upon an officer, there is no doubt that the effect on the prisoners is most decidedly preventive, and causes a man who knows the consequences to think twice before attacking a warder. As to the general effect upon the men themselves, much depends upon the character of the man so punished. Some it hardens, but others are undoubtedly benefited by it.

I remember one case in particular. He was in many respects a decent sort of man, and always ready for a chat with the chaplain, but he was always getting reported for some fault or another, and I constantly found him under punishment for some months. Again and again I reasoned with him, and told him what a fool he was to carry on in this way. At last I said, What you are working up for is a sound flogging, and youll get it for certain, if you don't turn over a new leaf." Shortly afterwards my prophecy was fulfilled, and he was sentenced to two dozen with the birch for a more serious offence than usual. All the time he was undergoing the punishment he was reading himself a lecture as to his folly and misconduct. This is just what you deserve, James; it is what the chaplain told 204 A CHAPLAIN ON DAKTMOOK you you would get. I hope, like a sensible fellow, you will lay it to heart, and turn over a new leaf," etc., etc, repeating his regrets over a misspent past and reproaching himself for his folly all the time the birch was being applied. I saw him in his cell next day, and found him by no means cast down. He said that it was just what I told him would be the end of the road he was travelling, and that it had brought him to his senses, and he meant in future to give up his tricks: and he did. He was never under report again.

In this case the improvement in the man's conduct was manifest, and it was lasting. Perhaps you will object that this was an exceptional case; but even one such affords a strong argument for the continuance of what on the face appears a cruel kind of punishment, and although much might be urged for its suppression, I think if we consider the warders and their safety, it ought to be continued. At the same time I believe in a more enlightened age not only will flogging cease, but all imprisonment such as is now in vogue will be abolished. The money it costs to keep the men for years in prison if spent instead to keep them out of prison would be sufficient and more than sufficient for the purpose. Think of the cost of the police employed to catch the criminal, and put him in prison, and the cost of his maintenance and supervision when in prison; add to this the cost of our police courts, and the sum total is more than sufficient to support the whole criminal population in affluence. This you will say is an Utopian suggestion, and would only encourage idleness. As the men are to-day it would not work, but if only part of this money were spent in the prevention of crime, instead of at a later date in the criminal's punishment and reformation, I believe the time would soon arrive when the number of prisoners would so diminish that our prisons might be closed.

There has been a discussion lately in the papers as to the advantage or otherwise of clergymen wearing a suitable dress, so that they carry on them the outward and visible sign of their calling, in the black coat and white tie, descendants of the cassock and clerical stock. It is said on the one hand that the advantages outweigh the disadvantages. That wherever he goes a clergyman ought to be known as such, and that in the case of a sudden call to the bedside of 206 A CHAPLAIN ON DARTMOOR a sick person he ought to carry on his person the emblems of his office. On the other hand, it is said to mark him out, and dissociate him from his fellow-men, so producing an insuperable barrier, and creating a sort of exclusiveness, so spoiling any chance of real social intercourse. Then it is said, how can a clergyman on holiday enjoy himself, clothed in black, and with a stiff white dog collar fastened round his nock, especially in the hot weather? He is a marked man, and is thus hampered if he, like his fellow-man, strolls into a bar for a glass of beer, or is seen taking part in some mild amusements which may be regarded as quite harmless for the laity. It may be only a matter for each man to decide for himself, only he must be aware that, let him discard his clerical attire in the holidays, or at any other time, he will not by that simple expedient disguise himself sufficiently to pass for a layman. He carries with him in his carriage, and bearing, and face, the unmistakeable marks of a parson. If I am walking on the promenade at any fashionable watering place I may meet many men in light tweeds or flannels, with a coloured tie, or no tie at all; in five cases out of six I should be pretty certain as to which of them were parsons in disguise. All this digression brings me to the personal equation. For my own part I always wear my white dog collar, emblem of my profession, for no higher reason than that it is more comfortable and easy than any other I know of. I must, however, candidly confess that I can only recall one occasion when it has been of any real service, and it came about in this wise.

There is a small branch railway in Cornwall which runs from the main line up to the Caradoc clay works, some eight miles up the hills, and tourists at the time I am thinking of were allowed to travel in these open trucks through very pretty scenes, overshadowed by trees all up the single track. On one occasion I made this trip in company with a lot of other trippers. Seated on the wooden plank opposite me was a pleasant young fellow, with whom I got into conversation. " Ever been up this way before? " he said. " No, I am quite a stranger to these parts," I replied. "Well he said, "the accommodation is limited to one small inn, and eatables are not over-abundant, so it is a case of first come first served, and the last go without. Now, this ramshackle bus runs right on to the clay works, 208 A CHAPLAIN ON DAETMOOR about a mile from the inn, but before it gets there it will slacken speed or stop for a minute, about the nearest place to the inn. When it does so I shall jump down and make for the inn, before the crowd who will go on to the terminus have time to follow. If you are wise, and hungry, you had better follow me." This I did, in the company of about a dozen others, who evidently knew the ropes. I was leading the way with my acquaintance, and the rest close behind, when we reached the door of the inn, where the landlady met us with a smiling welcome and ushered us upstairs, and into a nice airy guest chamber-There we found a table spread with an unusual supply of chickens and ham and other delicacies. We were not long in taking our places, knowing that a hungry mob would soon be arriving from the train. We had nearly finished when there appeared at the door a very clerical-looking gentleman, very angry and protesting very forcibly with the landlady, who was explaining to the irate cleric that when this gentleman (pointing to me at the head of the table) arrived with the rest of those at the table, she naturally mistook me in my white choker for his reverence. It turned out that he was a Roman Catholic

Canon from Plymouth, with his choir, and he had telegraphed the day before for dinner to be provided, which we had forestalled. He was naturally very angry, and although I apologised profusely for my unintentional mistake, he was not appeased, neither did the place provide further nourishment beyond the very plainest fare. It was the white tie that did it, as in other respects no one, certainly not a landlady, would mistake me for a Eoman Catholic Canon, although my companions might pass muster for a choir.

On another occasion I remember we had a visit from two gentlemen, who came armed with authority from the Home Office to be shown all over the prison; they were evidently big pots and the governor was, as usual, politeness itself. Accordingly he handed them over to a subordinate to be conducted round the buildings and workshops. When ttey had gone I asked the governor what they thought of all they had seen and what did they say about it all. " I don't know," he said; but their departure led to rather an amusing incident, which he narrated.

The reader must remember that there are two kinds of cats. One has nine tails, the other only 210 A CHAPLAIN ON DAKTMOOR one, and both have their uses in our penal establishments. One for the punishment of serious offences, such as assaulting warders, and the other for keeping down the rats, which seem to flourish on prison fare–as do the cats who feed on the rats, and consequently grow to an abnormal size. In fact, I have never seen finer animals or handsomer; consequently they are more admired than their namesakes with a larger number of tails.

When these two gentlemen, after inspecting the prison and the prisoners, came back to the governor's office to say good-bye and thank him for his civility to them, he said, "Well, I hope the attendant showed you all that is to be seen; is there anything more that you would like to look at? Sometimes we forget something."

" If it is allowed, we should much like to see a cat."

" Certainly," replied the governor; they are kept in a sealed-up packet in the steward's office. Ill send for one and he rang the bell.

When a warder appeared he said, "Oh, Williams, these gentlemen would like to see a cat, go and fetch one from the steward's office."

After some delay, and no return of the warder with cat, the bell was rung again, and another warder was despatched to hurry up the return of the first. Another delay, and a third warder was sent to tell the others to hurry up, as the gentlemen had to catch a train.

" Oh, please don't mind," they said, " it doesn't matter if there is any difficulty. Perhaps the steward has not got one in stock; it is a good sign, it shows you don't often want to use them."

After waiting some time longer, into the office burst three hot and dishevelled warders, with two of our splendid cats in their arms, apologising for the delay with the excuse that they couldn't catch them until after a long chase all over the yards. I do not know what the end of it was, but it was a very natural mistake on the part of the warders, who took a pride in the four-legged animal, but with difficulty could understand that anyone would care to see the cat-o'-nine-tails.

CHAPTER VIII.

PRISON LIFE–THE PRISON FARM.

ABOUT the year 1850 the authorities were somewhat troubled in mind what to do with the superabundance of our convicts. The Australians had begun to give polite hints to our Government that they thought their country might be put to a better purpose than as a dumping ground for our surplus of bad characters, and their objection came with the greater force in that the majority of the then well-to-do citizens, or their forefathers, once upon a time, years ago, had themselves come out there with a free passage at Government expense; but having long since served their time had now become prosperous citizens and strongly objected to receive other consignments of bad characters. So, as the Government could no longer wash their hands or save their pockets by transportation, they tried the plan of dumping the unfortunate convicts on board ship, and keeping them there, anchored in our own harbours. This led to so many abuses and cost such a lot of money that it was decided to keep them on land, instead of immuring them on the hulks.

Sir Joshua Jebb was the head of the prison department, and looking about for a suitable abode for our criminal population, he fixed upon the old, deserted, empty prison on Dartmoor. There was at least the shell, and with some little labour it might be furbished up to hold a few hundred prisoners. The site was healthy, far removed from other habitations of honest people, and once located it would be a difficult place for prisoners to escape from, being somewhat like an island, surrounded by miles of moorland instead of water.

So in the year I have named steps were taken to repair and rebuild the old prison; a number of men were marched up from the hulks at Plymouth, and in a short time made the prison habitable, and also put the old barracks in fit order for the dwelling-places of warders and a few soldiers.

I knew the first governor who was appointed to carry out this work and see that none of the convicts made their escape. It was an anxious 214 A CHAPLAIN ON DARTMOOR and heavy responsibility for any man, and required great tact and ability. He was a very kind and humane gentleman, and succeeded in a few years in restoring the old prison and getting things in order. I was once talking to him about some of the disadvantages of life on the moor in the year 1880.

" Ah! " he said, looking round, "I wish you had been with me when I came here to take charge in 1850; you would think little of the present drawbacks. There was then no prison farm, with its milk and butter at a small cost. There was no railway nearer than Plymouth. No shops; in fact, there was nothing, unless we fetched it from Tavistock or Plymouth. Nothing but moorland, and very bad roads."

All this was in striking contrast to present-day surroundings. Three new prisons, spacious warders' quarters, nice and commodious houses for the officials, emporiums in the village where you can buy anything from hair pins to evening dresses, and a good service of trains to Plymouth, not counting the supplies to be obtained from the farm and gardens.

What would the first officials have thought if they could have seen a little into the future?

Now we have our reading room, a billiard table, and a large recreation room where in the winter evenings our dramatic society give us some of the best and most amusing modern plays. Coming away from one or other of our great soirees, with dancing in full swing, and making my way across the road to my quarters in a howling snow-storm, I have sometimes wondered if it was real, or only a dream, that such a scene of festivity and jollity could really be taking place here in the wilds of Dartmoor. Well, well, we may have some drawbacks to put up with, but certainly we have compensations in these dances and plays by night, and our cricket and tennis by day.

In the rebuilding of Dartmoor there was something to begin on, but that is not always the case. I watched from week to week the building of a great prison near London, where to begin with there was nothing but a green field, and only a muddy approach to the same, until I saw the building complete, and capable of holding in safety 1,500 prisoners and their attendant warders.

You will say, how is it done? Here is the problem; you have 500 or 1,000 men, every one of them anxious, if possible, to run away, and 216 A CHAPLAIN ON DAKTMOOR you want them to build a prison for their own safe custody! It is something like the puzzle of the man who wanted to transport over a river a fox, a goose, and a bag of corn, in a boat that would only hold one of the three at a time. If left alone the fox would eat the goose, and the goose would eat the corn. How was it done? Very easily and with no loss either to goose or corn. In like manner the big prison grew by degrees until it was finished, and there it stands, a monument of what men who very much dislike work, and will escape from it if they can, may do with a little compulsion and supervision.

Such were my thoughts when I found myself hoisted high above London in the big wheel and looked down upon Wormwood Scrubbs prison. I thought of my first visit with the doctor, who went there weekly to see any complaining sick, when as a beginning there were only about a dozen cells completed. To build a new prison, with prison work, at first only a few men are employed, until cells are constructed on the bare field in which these workmen are at first confined. Gradually more are added, and as the number increases, so does the work, and in time a five-storied building is complete, with its 300 cells and a roof to cover all.

There are difficulties at first which do not arise with free workmen. For suppose something has been forgotten, a hammer or chisel, you can't say to your prisoner, "Just cut back and fetch it as the probability is you would see neither tool or workman again. I have frequently known this to happen in my own quarters; a party of prisoners in charge of two or three warders arrive after breakfast to do some repairs in the house, a door or window sash. The men arrive looking pleased and ready for the job. There is a great flourish unpacking tools and materials, when someone finds out that he has forgotten to bring a certain tool from the workshop, without which the work cannot proceed; what is the consequence? The whole party must pack up everything, march back to the prison and fetch the forgotten tool. By the time they return half the morning is gone, and the less work done.

This may be of small consequence when it happens near the prison, but how if it is far from the prison from whence they come, and the first start in building a new prison. Nor can the difficulty be got over by sending someone else for the missing tool. I remember in one case 218 A CHAPLAIN ON DARTMOOR when this was done, but I don't think the warder would repeat it. He had charge of a party who were doing some repairs upstairs in the governor's quarters. The governor's wife came up to see, and give some directions, with her baby in her arms. Just then the men discovered that they had left a certain tool downstairs and were about to pack up, and all tramp down to fetch it. A happy idea occurred to the good lady, and she volunteered to go downstairs and fetch the missing tool if the warder would hold the baby until her return. This would save time, and as she knew the warder to be a family man, she handed over the baby to him without any misgiving. Unfortunately for the warder the governor himself came on the scene, and of course questioned the warder as to the baby in his arms. It was, of course, a serious breach of discipline, and although it was his own kid, he fined the warder five shillings for the offence. I don't know, but I strongly suspect the good lady paid that fine, and the warder learned a lesson without loss to his pocket.

The prison farm is an important part of the establishment, and affords a pleasant and useful occupation for a large number of convicts. It has all been built by convict labour, and consists of stables, barns, a dairy, sheep pens, cow byres, and pigstyes. The stock yard is filled with a number of large ricks of hay, oats, barley, but no wheat, all gathered in from the fields that have been reclaimed from the moor by convict labour. The stock comprises a fine flock of sheep, a herd of 30 cows, ponies, horses, and pigs. Once a year there is an annual sale of the surplus stock, and good prices are fetched at auction from purchasers gathered from all parts of Devon and other counties, the prison stock being noted far and wide for its excellent quality. As much as 1,500 has been paid into the prison treasury in a year, the most satisfactory return in the accounts on the debit side of the balance sheet.

It is an interesting sight to see the convicts at lambing time tending and feeding the lambs, old Davies, the Dartmoor shepherd, being one of the best foster parents amongst the dozen or so employed. He was released before the expiration of his sentence at the intercession of Messrs. Lloyd George and Churchill when they paid a visit to the prison, but was soon afterwards welcomed back by the farm staff when he returned on a fresh sentence.

220 A CHAPLAIN ON DARTMOOR

The dairy produce was much appreciated by the officials, who were supplied at market prices with such butter and milk as they could obtain nowhere else, the milkmaid, or dairy woman, being the only member of the prison staff of the female sex. In times of scarcity, owing to snowstorms cutting us off from all trade with Tavi-stock or Plymouth, the slaughter of the prison pigs more than once saved us from famine.

I was once showing a friend round the farm building when he called my attention to an incident I had never noticed before. It was near closing time, and the recall bell began ringing, at the sound of which the men left off work and began to fall in for their return to the prison. Just then in through the gate leading to the field beyond the yard rushed a whole herd of swine. Placed along the side of the yard were a number of pigstyes with a closed door to each, and as the pigs trooped in to the yard, each halted at the door of his own sty (cell I was going to write) until the warder went along and opened each door, admitted the occupant, and closed it again on him. Well," said my friend, "I never saw anything like that." " Like what? " I exclaimed. Why each pig knows his own abode."

The warder, hearing him, said, "Oh yes, they know their own location as well as the prisoners; they never make a mistake. If you had seen them feeding in the field outside you would have seen something funnier still." What was that? " said my friend. Why as soon as that recall bell began ringing they all left off feeding and came down to the gate; they know there's something better in their styes than grass; listen to the row they are making with their noses in the swill."

Our farm bailiff was an enterprising, clever Scotchman, who took great interest in the stock. He had got the prison sheep to such a high pitch of excellence that he carried off most of the prizes at all the county shows; and the flock as a whole was one to be proud of. Sometimes his zeal led him to make mistakes. I was talking to him in the road one day when there passed us a number of black sheep. I remarked on the unusual number, and said if they were all born on the farm it was a curious coincidence considering how many black sheep of the two-legged we already had on the establishment. " No," he said, " they were not dropped by our own ewes; I have bought them here and there from 222 A CHAPLAIN ON DAETMOOR neighbouring farmers." " Whatever for? " I said, " are they better than ordinary coloured ones? I always thought they were inferior." Then he told me the secret, that Lady M., in Scotland, had found that by mixing the natural wool of white and black she could obtain an excellent blend of colour that required no dye of any kind, and that it proved of far more value than the dyed yarns. " I am going to give it a trial," he said. I never learned the result, but as in course of time the flock of black sheep disappeared, I suppose the experiment was a failure. Let us hope that the same may happen with the other flock of black sheep, and prisons will no longer be wanted in which to fold them, and the shepherd will find other sheep and the flock other pastures.

CHAPTER IX.

EX-CONVICTS

DURING my many years of service in the prison, thousands of men must have passed under my care, and thousands must be scattered over the country, enjoying their liberty in town or country; and so small is the world of England, it is not surprising that many meetings, in most unexpected places and times, happen between their old chaplain and his former charges. Go where I will, I have met them to the mutual pleasure and satisfaction of both parties–in the remotest country places, at railway stations, in theatres, and more frequently in the streets of London.

I was once riding my bicycle down the Wye valley, when a man jumped up from a heap of stones upon which he had been sitting, and accosted me with the cry, "Oh! Mr. R., who would have thought of seeing you here? Don't you know me? Why I used to sing in your 224 A CHAPLAIN ON DARTMOOR choir in the prison chapel." I dismounted, and over a pipe we talked over old times, and discussed his future prospects. He said he was tramping the country and looking for work. Yes," I said, " looking for work and hoping you won't find it!:

On another occasion I was leaning out of the carriage window whilst the train stopped at Salisbury, when a well-groomed gentleman passed along the platform, and as I just glanced at him, to my surprise, he saluted with his hand to his hat, and then passed on. Reaching the end of the platform he turned and retraced his steps, and when about to pass me a second time, repeated his salutation and paused with the remark: " You don't seem to recognise me, chaplain; why I was sweeping your chimney at Dartmoor a few months ago!: Well," I said, " you don't look much like a chimney-sweep to-day, so you mustn't be surprised if I failed to recognise an old acquaintance. I suppose you have retired from your former very useful profession; what are you doing now?: " I am a commercial traveller now," he said. " I see you are a traveller, but the commerce is, I am afraid, doubtful." He smiled and wished me good-day. It was no wonder that I failed to recognise him. When last I saw him he was dressed in the hideous yellow dress with its broad arrows, and no beard and very little hair. Now he was dressed in well-fitting frock coat, with a flower in his button-hole, a shining top hat, and well-trimmed black beard and moustache.

Kather an amusing thing happened to me in an unexpected meeting with an old convict in London. I had emerged from the underground railway at Portland Road station, with two small boys I was convoying for a day at the Zoo, when the first person I met in the street was an old convict I had said good-bye to on his release from prison only the week before. I stopped him and made kind enquiries as to his health and welfare, but as there were a good many people about I took his arm and invited him to walk with me in the park, where we could have a little talk. As we walked towards the gates, we met a policeman, who, I saw by his look, recognised my friend, and when he had passed on a few yards he turned and shadowed us through the gates, and into the park. When we had gone half way towards the Zoo I said good-bye to my friend, who scurried off across the grass, and 226 A CHAPLAIN ON DARTMOOR disappeared. But not so the policeman, who knew where he could find an ex-convict, but not the friend who appeared to be so intimate, and might therefore be not unknown to the police, and so he followed me right up to the entrance gates of the Zoo, and then we parted. I wish I could have read that policeman's thoughts.

Other mistakes have been made in regard to my status. I wonder sometimes whether one carries the smell or taint of prison, regardless of one's position as officer or prisoner. I was for a time doing duty in a charming parish in Herefordshire, and one afternoon was salmon fishing on a likely pool on the Wye, where I was joined by a wild-looking man of the woods, who after enquiring after the sport, and giving me advice, appeared to be getting rather too familiar and friendly. " Is it true," he asked, " what they tell me, that you have come from Dartmoor? I was there myself for more than ten years, but you must have done your time since I left; I don't think I ever saw you there." He was quite anxious to help me, and offered to row me in his boat. I told him it was quite true that I had come from the prison, and found life elsewhere so dull that I intended shortly to go back there. He seemed surprised and exclaimed, Things must have altered very much since my time. Fancy anyone wanting to go back there! " I was not in clerical attire, but in old fishing clothes and waders, hence I suppose his mistake. Did I carry the prison taint about me?

CHAPTER X.

A MIDNIGHT ADVENTURE I HAVE some hesitation in describing my midnight encounter with a burglar, lest I should be open to the charge of boasting of my capture of a man who had been guilty of a whole series of burglaries before he got into my house, and unfortunately for himself ran up against me, in the course of his wandering from one room to another in search of plunder. Full accounts of the burglary appeared at the time in most of the papers, most of them fairly accurate, some a little distorted. The following is the correct version so far as I can recall the incident after a lapse of 25 years.

It was on Sunday night, in March, 1895, that being unable to sleep when I got to bed and after lying awake for an hour or two, I thought I would get up and go down to my study, and compose myself with a book and a pipe. I determined to do this, as I thought I heard my

A MIDNIGHT ADVENTURE 229 wife moving in the room below. She was sleeping in a bedroom adjacent to the one I was occupying, with a young girl who at the time was unwell, and I concluded she had gone downstairs to fetch something for her. With this idea in my head, I slipped on a dressing gown over my pyjamas and descended the stairs expecting to find my wife. I noticed as I went down that the door leading down to the kitchen was open, and as it was closed when I went up to bed, I concluded that my wife had gone down to fetch some milk for the invalid. When I reached the hall at the bottom of the stairs I noticed a light shining through the open door of my study, and thought to myself, "Whatever does she want in there? J: never for a moment imagining there was anybody else in the room.

As I proceeded along the passage or hall a man came hurriedly through the door of the study, carrying a lighted candle in one hand and an open long knife in the other. He was dressed in the conventional burglar style, a muffler round his neck, short jacket, corduroy trousers, and a rakish cloth cap sideways on his head. He came out so suddenly that in meeting we almost knocked up against each other, and before 230 A CHAPLAIN ON DARTMOOE I had time to realise who or what it was I had met instead of my expected wife, he raised the open knife over my head and uttered two or three extraordinary yells, something like the war-whoop of an American Indian. There was no escape for either of us, if we were so minded, as we were almost touching each other. As he was making his noises, no doubt with the idea of frightening me, I took hold of his coat collar and led him into the study, at the same time saying to him, "Stop that fooling and come in here." In the study I sat on the table and stood him beside me. I asked him what he had got to say for himself, and what he was doing in my house at that time of night. He replied, "I only wanted something to eat, and a bit to go on with, govnor; you won't give me up, will you?: I replied, "I don't know about that; what's the use of letting you go, youll only break into somebody else's house." He assured me that never again would he do such a thing; " but look here," he said, "I won't be took."

All this time he was handling the open knife, and seeing this, I said, "Look here, we shall get on better if you give me that knife," at the same time I took hold of it and tried to take it from

A MIDNIGHT ADVENTURE 231 him. He would not release it, and in the scuffle I got badly cut through two ringers, and bear the scars to this day. In the scrimmage I found myself on the inside of the room near the fireplace, the man between me and the door. I did not relish the change in his demeanour, as he was now rather threatening, brandishing the knife in front of me and repeating his cry, "I won't be took, I won't be took at any price." I kept the table between us, and noticing my gun leaning against the wall I suddenly reached over and snatching it up I pulled the hammer to full cock and said, What's that you say? You certainly will be took, my friend."

He blew out his candle and bolted from the room, stooping low as he ran through the door into the passage, as though he thought I might shoot at him. The gun, however, was, of course, unloaded; so I went to a drawer and took out two cartridges loaded with small shot for snipe and then set out in search of the man, although I did not expect to see him again, as I naturally concluded he would get out of the house by the same way he came in. I went first into the dining room, but he was not there, and was about to go down and explore the kitchen when I heard 232 A CHAPLAIN ON DARTMOOR a slight noise in the drawing-room, and stepping in discovered my friend at the far end of the long room trying to unfasten the window. This had double windows, which evidently puzzled him, and so putting my candle on the table I went a few steps into the room and raising the gun to my shoulder I said, "Now then, bail up, Billy, or Ill blow your head off!: Instead of doing so he came straight down the room with his head bent and brandishing the knife in his hand. I did not like to shoot, and so when he nearly reached me, I stepped further into the room and as he passed me for the door, I made a sweep with the gun and thought I hit him with the barrels on the nape of his neck. (In an interview I had with him afterwards, when we amicably discussed the incidents of the evening, he said that I missed him, as he stooped and so evaded the blow.) He disappeared through the door and made back for the study, I following close on his heels. Why he did not run down into the kitchen I do not know, but I think he must have lost his head.

Reaching the study, I found him standing on the hearthrug; I stood in the open doorway, and putting my candle on the table, again called to

A MIDNIGHT ADVBNTUKE 233 him to bail up, that the gun was loaded and I should certainly shoot if he tried to approach. " Put that knife down and bail up," I repeated. Instead of doing so he brandished the knife, and swore he wasn't going to be took. As he seemed bent on mischief, I cried again to him, "Keep back, the gun is loaded and I shall fire." He took no notice, but appeared to be coming at me, and so very reluctantly I pulled the trigger, aiming as I thought at his hand with the knife in it. The gun must have thrown up a bit, as the charge caught him in the forearm, and falling on to the hearthrug he called out, "Youve shot me through the heart." I put down the gun, and went over to him, and getting some whisky administered a pretty strong dose. The noise of the gun woke up the house, and I heard my wife from the landing calling out, "What's the matter, what are you doing? " " Ive got a burglar here, and Ive shot him." " Oh, I hope you haven't hurt him!!! " The servants came tumbling down, half dressed, and soon we had two doctors, two or three warders, and the policeman in attendance. The doctors bound up the man's arm, and ordered his removal at once to the Tavistock hospital–although I asked 234 A CHAPLAIN ON DARTMOOR them to put him to bed upstairs– where he was conveyed by the policeman and a warder in a carriage from the hotel. Arrived there he was seen by four doctors, who decided that the arm must be amputated below the elbow, which was accordingly done, and after six weeks in hospital he was conveyed to Exeter and tried before Judge Vaughan Williams.

Two days after the shooting I went down to the hospital, where I was allowed an interview with the man. I sat down by his bedside and at first he would take no notice of me. It appears several people had been to see him, with a view to identifying him for various burglaries, and no doubt he thought I was another visitor on the same errand.

I spoke quietly to him, and said I hoped he was going on all right, and then I said, "You don't seem to know me." With that he condescended to turn round, and looking at me said, f No, Ive never seen you before, don't know you." " Yes, you do," I said, "look again. I'm the man youve got to thank for this, and I'm very sorry it has happened. Tell me, now, why didn't you give in when I told you to hands up." " I didn't like the look of you, " he said. " Well,

A MIDNIGHT ADVENTURE 235 but I told you the gun was loaded." " I didn't think you would shoot he said. We then had quite a friendly chat, and discussed the various incidents of the previous Sunday night. He told me that he came to Princetown without intending it, that he was on the main Plymouth road, at Eoborough Down, and being misdirected he took the turning towards Dowsland, and did not discover his mistake until he found himself at Princetown. Here he went to the police station, and asked the policeman where he could get a lodging for the night. He was told he must go to Tavistock; and the policeman accompanied him as far as Rundlestone and showed him the road leading to Tavistock. It was curious that the policeman did not recognise him (I wish he had) as a man that had been wanted for some time for various burglaries, and whose description had been circulated throughout the county, and was in the hands of every policeman. Having shown him the way, the policeman returned home by the high road, but the man wasn't going to walk another seven miles, and so he told me that as soon as the policeman left him he got over a wall and doubled back, through the fir plantations that run parallel with the road, 236 A CHAPLAIN ON DARTMOOR and end just at my garden wall. He got over this, inspected my front garden, and was attracted to the iron fence enclosing the area of the front of the house, with a drop of about eight feet to a well in front of the kitchen windows. He dropped into this, and forced the window by inserting his knife and pushing back the catch, so that he could then raise the window and climb in. Much to his satisfaction the servants had left a good fire burning. He warmed himself, and then taking off his boots, which he placed on the table, he next proceeded to the pantry and made a selection from the eatables, took them to the kitchen fire, and there ate his supper in comfort. Then lighting his candle he went upstairs and ransacked the drawers in my writing table, but found nothing worth stealing. He then went into the study, and coming out, to his surprise, almost ran up against me; then he said, "You know what happened then." I did. I told him that it so happened I had more money that night in my writing table than usual, and I wondered he had not found it. He replied that he would have had it, if I had not interfered, as he was on his way back to have another search in the dining-

A MIDNIGHT ADVENTURE 237 room when lie met me. He said that he only got in to get something to eat, and didn't mean to do me any harm! " Then why did you cut my two fingers like that? " I said, showing him my bandaged hand with arm in sling. That was your own fault," he said, " in trying to take the knife away from me." " But why did you not give it up when I seized it? " "I didn't like the look of you," he said, " and I wasn't going to be took." " But," I said, " why didn't you get away out of the house, the same way that you came in, after you left me in the study?" " I don't know," he said, "I missed my way and was not sure of the way out, and I knew you were close after me with a loaded gun." " Did you know the gun was loaded? " I asked. " Yes," he said, "I heard you put the cartridges in, and the click of the barrels. Ive been a soldier and know."

It seemed curious to me at the time, but very natural and interesting, to be sitting there close by his bedside, and quietly talking the matter over in the most friendly manner, when only forty-eight hours before we were at deadly grips. The poor fellow was in a bad way, and when I told him how sorry I was to have been 238 A CHAPLAIN ON DARTMOOR obliged to fire, and so injure him that his life was in danger, he replied, "That's all right; it was my fault, and I forgive you."

It does not often happen, I think, that an interview so affecting between robber and robbed takes place. Well," I said, "I hope you will soon be all right again; mind and do whatever the doctor tells you, and I will do all I can to get you off any further punishment." He thanked me and we parted like two friends.

I called at the hospital again several times, but I was not allowed to see him. The next time I saw him was when he was brought before the magistrates at Tavistock, when I asked them to deal summarily with the man, as I thought they would agree that he had been sufficiently punished for what he had done. The Clerk informed us that it was not in their power to do so, and that he must be committed for trial at the Exeter sessions. This was accordingly done, and the next day he was taken to Ivybridge and in like manner committed to the same assizes for two burglaries to which he pleaded guilty, and which had taken place a week previous to my encounter. Accordingly on the following June 17th we met again at the Guildhall at Exeter before Judge kvaughan Williams and a jury.

A MIDNIGHT ADVENTURE 239

The prisoner was brought in to the crowded court, and was charged with the two burglaries at Ivy bridge, and also with the burglary at Princetown. He pleaded " guilty " to the first two counts, but " not guilty " to the latter. " Not guilty to the one at Pricetown? " said counsel in surprise. Yes," said the prisoner, "Not guilty; I want to be tried." This was done because if he pleaded guilty to this there would have been no evidence needed, and he thought that I should have had no opportunity to beg him off. So the trial proceeded and my evidence and that of the other witnesses taken, after which the prisoner was asked by the judge, "Do you wish to ask the witnesses any questions before the jury give their verdict? " " Yes, I do," replied the prisoner. The judge then warned the man that it would be better for him if he left the matter as it was. f I have generally found," he said, " that prisoners who avail themselves of this privilege more often than not do themselves more harm than good by asking questions; however, if you still wish to do so proceed."

Prisoner: When I met you at the bottom of the stairs.

240 A CHAPLAIN ON DARTMOOR

Judge: Stop, stop, what do you mean? You have pleaded " not guilty" to this charge. What stairs are you alluding to?

Prisoner: If I had liked could I have got the gun before you?

Rev. C. R.: Yes, certainly; but you could not have got the cartridges.

Prisoner: I didn't want to do you any harm. I only came in to lie down.

Rev. C. R.: I am glad to hear you say so.

I forget the rest of my cross-examination; but all the questions were enough to establish the prisoner's guilt, if there had been no other evidence.

After the Judge had summed up the jury retired, and shortly returned with a verdict of " guilty. 1 I then asked the judge's permission to speak a few words before sentence was passed, and then said, "I am not here to prosecute the unfortunate man for breaking into my house, but being subpoenaed by the police I was obliged to appear as a witness. I think the man has been sufficiently punished for what he did, and I hope your lordship will let him off with a light sentence."

The Judge said, "You want me to deal

A MIDNIGHT ADVENTURE 241 leniently with him? " " I want your lordship to let him ofi any further punishment if you can do so."

The judge intimated that he would postpone sentence until the next day.

When the prisoner was brought up for sentence, the Judge remarked: " I think we are old acquaintances, are we not? Were you not tried before me at Chester? J:

Prisoner: I thought you was the gentleman, sir (laughter).

The Judge: Well, you know you haven't quite kept your word with me. I don't say you have not tried to do so. You have a very Jong list of convictions against you indeed. You have been sent to penal servitude for a long time and you have been in prison for a long time. I thought it a pity that you should spend the latter part of your life in prison and so I only sent you to prison for six months. Isn't that so?

The Prisoner: Yes, sir.

The Judge: You said that if I did not send you to prison you would be quite sure never to get into prison again. Here you are once more; but still I am happy to say you must have tried a little to carry out your promise, because your 242 A CHAPLAIN ON DARTMOOR conviction before me was on the 30th November, 1891. Now it is 1895, so that you seem to have kept out of mischief for some time; but on this particular evening that you were taken, whatever it was you intended to do in the chaplain's house you had already committed a burglary about the same time in somebody else's house. So you began your dishonest habits again. I only mention this to you in the hope that you will now keep out of prison. I daresay you will find it more difficult to do anything now you have lost your arm. But I do not doubt that you will be able to keep out of prison if you choose. It is better at your time of life even to be in the workhouse than in the prison, but I hope you may keep out of both. Now you have lost your arm– and you lost it in the commission of this crime–I have no doubt that has put you to a great deal of pain, and I therefore do not propose to pass any serious punishment on you. The chaplain had no intention of hurting you more than was necessary for the defence of his house and he is very sorry that in defending himself, as he was perfectly justified in doing, the result was that your arm was so shot that it had to be amputated; and he has asked me to deal

A MIDNIGHT ADVENTURE 243 mercifully with you. Therefore I propose to do so. I dare say that in the present state of your arm you are not able to do much work. Under these circumstances I shall only order you to be imprisoned for one month. It will be with hard labour, because I think you will get better food by that."

I was glad to find the Judge was inclined to deal so leniently with him and immediately took steps to provide some honest occupation for him, at the end of the month, and, with the help of a few friends interested in the man, a sum sufficient to provide for his keep for some time, and to start him in business as a fish hawker was raised. He was sent to Bath, there to be under the wing, if I remember right, of the Church Army. Before the money was all spent he disappeared altogether, leaving no clue to his intentions.

It was not until the following October that we again heard of him. Then news came that there had been several burglaries committed by a man in Shropshire, and it was thought that the man arrested was the Princetown burglar. A request came to me from the police to send a photograph of my burglar, if I had one, as the man denied that he was the Princetown burglar.

244 A CHAPLAIN ON DARTMOOR I had the photo, but declined to send it. I had had enough of the business, and declined to have anything further to do with the case. Accordingly our policeman was sent for, and easily identified the man when he was placed amongst a number of men. When he was leaving the prison he met the governor, who, on learning that he had identified the man, said, "Did you speak to

him? " " No, sir, I did not." " Oh, then," said the governor, let us go to his cell and hear what he has to say; perhaps he will own up now he has seen you."

On entering the cell he was greeted by the prisoner, "Good-evening, Mr. C. How are you? and how is the chaplain? " " Well," said the governor,: why didn't you own to the fact without giving us all this trouble? " "I thought I might as well have a run for my money."

In due time he was arraigned on six charges of burglary, and when the charges were made he replied, "I plead guilty to the first two and not guilty to the others." The prosecuting counsel said at once that as prisoner had pleaded guilty to two of the indictments he did not intend to proceed with the others. His lordship assented to this. (Why was not this course adopted at

A MIDNIGHT ADVENTURE 245

Exeter when the prisoner acted in the same manner?)

Police Constable Crispin, of the Devon constabulary, who said he was stationed at Prince-town, then said, "On the 17th of June last prisoner was convicted at the Exeter assizes for burglary at the residence of the chaplain at Dartmoor Prison. He was shot by the chaplain and wounded in the left arm. On prisoner's discharge from Exeter Prison the chaplain at Dartmoor and several other gentlemen subscribed a sum of money and started Brennan as a fish hawker at Bath. One month's board and lodging was paid for him and if he went on all right he was to have another month's board and lodging. He remained at Bath for a fortnight and then suddenly disappeared. Nothing more was heard of him until he was arrested in Shropshire for burglary."

His lordship in passing sentence said it was quite clear prisoner was one of those men for whom nothing could be done and from whom nothing could be expected. He had had a long career of crime (his various sentences named), and lastly, at Exeter in 1895, one month for burglary. Prisoner on that occasion received

246 A CHAPLAIN ON DARTMOOR one month only, his lordship supposed, because in prosecuting the burglary prisoner received severe wounds. A number of kind gentlemen tried to find him means to earn an honest living, but he deliberately abandoned the career held out to him, and returned to a life of crime. He had wandered about the country committing crime, and it was quite absurd to treat him in any way but as a very hardened criminal, whose desire to reform was absolutely hopeless. For the present offence to which he had pleaded guilty prisoner would have to go to penal servitude for six years.

The last news I had of him was from the visit of an old convict, who when at liberty always paid me a yearly visit, wherever I might be living. He walked all the way from London, and I was usually prepared for his visit by letters from the various clergymen upon whom he called on his way tome, and to whom he announced the object of his long walk of 250 miles, no doubt with the hope of getting a little assistance. The last time he came I thought by his manner that he had something more than usually interesting to tell me, so after somewhat beating about the bush, I said, "Well, Tommy, what is it? " " Well,"

A MIDNIGHT ADVENTURE 247 he said, "I daresay you remember Mollott, who broke into your house when we were both at Princetown, and he got more than he bargained for." " Yes," I said, "I remember, and I saw you amongst the spectators at the trial. What of it? " Yes, I was there, with a broken head, which I got the night before in a public-house row. Well, sir, not long since I was sent back to Parkhurst Prison for a few months for not reporting myself. I was working at the same bench as Mollott, and I told him that I was at his trial at Exeter and that you were a great friend of mine, and that I always paid you a visit when I was at liberty. Do you, he said, well, take a message for me to the chaplain and tell him that when I am out of prison I shall pay him another visit. I mean to call and see him again! " " Well, Tommy," I said, "I hope you will never go back to Parkhurst, but if you do, or meet Mollott anywhere, you can tell him this, I shall be glad to see him, but next time he comes he had better come in the daylight, and not at 1 o'clock in the morning."

Many of our convicts are more to be pitied than blamed, and if we knew how they were reared in the haunts of crime and encouraged 248 A CHAPLAIN ON DARTMOOR from earliest days to steal, we should be inclined to repeat John Bradford's remark when he saw a murderer being led to execution, "There, but for the grace of God, goes John Bradford."

" Well," you will say, " what can we do? " I suggest the following: get hold of the children and train them up in the right way. Pull down the slums. Stop the drink. Give every man the chance to work for a living wage, and when he is discharged from prison give the man a chance without interference by the police to earn an honest living, and encourage him in every way to work hard and so to recover his self-respect.

Lightning Source UK Ltd.
Milton Keynes UK

178744UK00001B/183/P

9 781154 821284